It took Charity a minute to realize that her assailant was Will. Then she struggled even harder. She was never going to let him take her back to that cabin.

"Charity, please. They're chasing us. You'll never be able to outrun them. We have to hide."

For a minute she only heard random sounds coming in between his panting breaths. Then the sounds formed words in her mind, and she was so surprised that she stopped struggling. He took advantage of her stillness to push her under the lip of a jutting rock.

"They're chasing me? You're the only one I see chasing me. You're in with some awful bunch of outliers."

"Hush, Charity, please. And be still. If we're quiet, they may go on by. We'll talk later."

"We won't ever talk again, Will Bowers. When I get back to Aunt Nell's—"

A hand, no longer gentle, covered her mouth. In the silence, she heard the crash of big feet running a little to the left of them. By the noise he was making smashing through bushes and starting rocks to rolling, she figured it must be the big man who had ridden behind her.

MARY LOUISE COLLN grew up in Illinois, but spent most of her adult life in Missouri. She wrote in her spare time while pursuing a nursing career and raising a family. She now writes full time in Franklin, Tennessee, where the natural beauty and sense of history encourage her fascination with the lives of our ancestors. She likes to write both historical and contemporary fiction.

Books by Mary Louise Colln

HEARTSONG PRESENTS
HP26—Mountain House
HP141—A Place for Love
HP228—Falling Water Valley

Birdsong Road

Mary Louise Colln

Heartsong Presents

To these strong and caring women:
Elaine, Nancy, Claire, Kelly, and Katie

A note from the author:
I love to hear from my readers! You may correspond with me
by writing: **Mary Louise Colln**
Author Relations
PO Box 719
Uhrichsville, OH 44683

ISBN 1-57748-619-6

BIRDSONG ROAD

Cover illustration by Dominick Saponaro.

PRINTED IN THE U.S.A.

prologue

Falling Water Valley, North Carolina
Written in June of the Year of Our Lord, 1865

My Dearest Niece,

I remember you as a child when my brother and
your dear father died. It may be that you don't
remember me at all. For that I blame myself. I have
let the difficult travel and my deep involvement in my
work here in the valley keep me from knowing my
Tennessee family.

I received a letter from someone who kept his or her
name secret but who must care for you. Perhaps it is
from a neighbor or a family friend. Whoever wrote
me, I thank them. The letter gave me news that you are
alone there, your lovely home burned and your mother
dead of a heart attack, your beloved brother not yet
back from the war. I refuse to believe anything but that
he will return as men from the valley here are return-
ing day by day. How we all have suffered from this
war and how much I thank God that it is finally over
and our lives can be picked up again with His help.

Charity Charlotte, this is the purpose of this letter.
I can't come to you for my husband (yes, I have married this late in life) and I are the only medical per-
sons to care for the people of the valley, with the help

5

*of my stepdaughter. I want with all my heart for you
to come to me. You will find the valley much different
from your home among those beautiful hills near
Nashville, for we are a much poorer people and live a
more difficult life. Even our social life is much different from what you are used to. We must depend on
each other and now we are finding it difficult to do
that because of our emotions.*

*But I don't mean to discourage you from coming to
me. We have much beauty here and, before the war
tore us apart, much love between neighbors. We hope
to rebuild that in the years to come. I must believe
that we can forget our divisions of Confederate and
Union and come together again, but I accept that it
may take years of effort.*

*And this brings me to the second reason for this let-
ter. Both our minister and our schoolteacher left the
valley during the war. My stepdaughter Bethany and
her future husband are working to get our church
open again, but we desperately need a teacher to
open our school.*

*I know that you have the background to teach our
children. We need you and want you here. The
Reverend Joshua Holt, who is our minister now, has
offered to bring you here if you will agree to come.
He knows people on the way and can bring you safely
through this still far from safe country. You can put
your trust in him as he is not only the minister working to bring our people together, he is also the future
husband of my stepdaughter.*

Please say that you will come to me. I am eagerly

awaiting your reply and, knowing how long it takes to get mail from me to you, I am already talking to the mothers of our children, who are eager to help you with the school.

> *Your loving aunt,*
> *Nell Morgan Andrews*
> *Written by Dr. Ben Andrews*

one

Charity Charlotte Morgan reached across the wooden slat seat of the old wagon and touched Joshua's arm.

"Stop a minute, please, Joshua."

Over the past days since Pastor Joshua Holt had, as a favor to Aunt Nell, brought her to North Carolina from her temporary home with friends near Nashville, they had moved to first names.

Joshua pulled the horses' reins to bring them to a stop. He stretched his long, booted legs for a moment before turning to her with an understanding smile. "A lot of the leaves are gone already and you can see some of the lower part of the valley from here now. High summer, about all you see is green leaves from here on up to the mountains. Later this winter you can even see some of the houses. Your aunt Nell lives smack up against the mountain at the top of the valley. We can't see that yet."

Charity couldn't pull up an answering smile. Discreetly, she stretched her own legs, too long to be comfortable in the low wagon seat, under cover of her well-worn linen skirt. The road leading into Falling Water Valley in the North Carolina mountains was covered with leaves, wet with wisps of fog, through which dark trunks of tall trees showed. Above, the bright mixture of green and gold led her gaze back off the road, past a few curls of fireplace smoke in the valley, to the blaze of color racing up the mountains. She watched the domineering bulk of the mountains for a few minutes. They seemed at the same time to tower over her and turn their backs on her. There was a remote beauty about it that Charity wasn't ready for, that she didn't find welcoming. She pulled her gaze closer to their wagon.

A black, dead tree with limbs twisted and twined back onto themselves, standing beside the wagon, seemed to her to symbolize her recent existence. She turned and looked at the pitifully flat canvas in the back of the wagon that held all that was left of her life before the late War Between the States, or, more accurately in Charity's mind, the War of Northern Aggression. Finally, she lifted her gaze back to the tops of the mountains rising up on both sides of the valley. She watched them for a while, then turned back to Joshua's sympathetic face.

"It's so different from Williamson County. The hills there hug you. These mountains dare you to love them."

He nodded. "But once you take the dare, you never get over loving them. You'll see. You may never want to go back to Middle Tennessee."

Charity didn't answer him directly. She couldn't imagine not ever wanting to get back life in the big house on acres of green land in Tennessee where she and Daniel and her mother had lived before the war. And where she had grown up in the tradition of society reserved for the daughters of wealthy and aristocratic families in Nashville and the surrounding plantations. She was sure that her mother must have carried sadness about her father's dying so young, but she didn't let Charity see it, and Charity's much older brother had run the farm and been like a father to her.

She pulled her mind back to Joshua. "What's the name of the road there?"

"You mean the main valley road? No name that I've ever heard," he answered. "They just call it the road. They've named some of the lanes that go down to the farms."

She took in a deep breath. "Then I'll name it to remember Williamson County. Birdsong Road."

He nodded. "It isn't always things we can hold in our hands that we bring with us when we move. Can we go on now? It's been a long, tiring journey and you need to get into your new home."

Charity clasped her hands. "Wait just a little." She felt each hand gripping the other. "I know Aunt Nell was Daddy's younger sister, but nobody has ever told me why she chose to stay here in the mountains. She sent me a sweet letter asking me to come live with her and her husband, but I don't remember her at all, even if she did come to visit us when Daddy died. I was too little then to remember."

"I promise you, Charity, that you will feel like you've known her all your life shortly after she takes you in her arms. Everyone feels that way about Nell Morgan Andrews. She birthed most all the young people of the valley."

"Even though her husband is a doctor?"

"Most of the women would rather have a woman with them. And Nell's been here always. Doc Andrews only came into the valley five or six years ago, then he was gone some in the war. No, Nell still does most of the births. And," he added, "after you get to know her, you will understand why she chose to spend her life helping people. She's a missionary who puts her messages in action, not words, like we long-winded preachers do."

He fidgeted with the reins.

Charity tried not to let him hear her sigh. She was tired after days of riding in the uncomfortable wagon and nights spent wherever Pastor Joshua found one of the families he had become acquainted with in his circuit riding days. But she dreaded having to adjust to change one more time.

She managed a small smile.

"I know why you want to go on, Joshua. You're anxious to see Bethany."

He returned her smile with a wide-open grin. "It's purely been awhile," he answered.

"All right. I will like my aunt. Let's go."

His grin widened. "That's the spirit. And it's true. You will not only like her, you will love her."

She nodded, using her fingers to try to smooth spiraling strands of her curly red hair and push them back under her small bonnet.

"Don't worry about that hair," Joshua admonished, giving her an affectionate look. "You're a mighty pretty eighteen-year-old and Miss Nell is going to love you right back. But she'd love you anyway, even if you were ugly as home-made sin."

"Thanks, Joshua." She knew that he didn't always speak in the down-to-earth comforting jargon he was using now. She had heard him deliver a sermon back in Williamson County while he was waiting for her to get her few things together and be ready to leave. Joshua Holt's goal was for his audience to be comfortable enough with his speaking to hear what he was saying.

"Perhaps we could say thank you to God for getting us here safely before we go on," he said.

She took his hand and sat quietly. There was much to be thankful for in any safe travel across Tennessee and North Carolina in 1865, when the roads were still full of unlawful men; returned soldiers who had lost all vestiges of Southern culture; bushwhackers, some of whom fought everybody, hoping to get the carpetbaggers who were changing the South forever in ways no one wanted, hoping to get even, or just taking advantage of the opportunity to get someone else's possessions as they had done during the late war.

She shuddered, remembering the night she had watched her own home burning, and thought again that the house might have survived being headquarters for a Union regiment if she had accepted a kiss from that captain instead of hitting him with a piece of firewood. But who could allow a kiss from one of the men who had made her brother leave and not be heard from again? Or caused her mother to have a heart attack and die early in the war?

Before she had finished her own thoughts, Joshua had murmured a few words to the Lord and jiggled the reins, starting up the horses. He let the two tired animals pull the wagon slowly up the almost imperceptibly rising road toward the head of the valley. But Charity wished they would take even more time to get there.

Joshua waved his hand to the right. "There's the school where you'll be teaching, over there."

Charity looked at the small, neglected-looking log building set back from the road amid tall, seed-topped grasses that dipped and swayed gently in the slight breeze. The noon sun, filtering through yellow-leafed trees, seemed to surround it with a honey glow that raised her spirits in spite of herself.

"See," Joshua said, watching her, "even our sugar maples want to welcome you. Makes you feel like God is right in there with you when you're under a bunch of them."

She only nodded and they went on past some cabins set barely back from the road and narrow lanes leading down to cleared areas where she could see glimpses of barns and spring houses. Here and there a cow wandered. She saw a woman stirring something in a big, black pot over an open fire and felt a flash of sympathy. The September day was warm and the woman's long dress seemed dangerously close to the fire.

Joshua kept up a running conversation without her doing more than murmur once in awhile, pointing at a lane or a cabin and calling out the name of someone who lived there. "Tabitha and Nathan Ballard live a little ways down there. I've stayed with them sometimes, but now I've moved into the house where Bethany and I will live after the wedding. It's set way back almost to the mountain. Just off the main road. . .just off Birdsong Road. . .there is Bertie McMillan and her little girl, Sally. Husband went off near the beginning of the war and was killed, so they live alone. There's an empty cabin over on the left here. That's where the church pastor lived before the war. It's been empty since he got scared at the beginning of the war. Run off by the bushwhackers. They despoiled this valley for a while. Worse than what the neighbors did to each other, fighting over who took to the Union and who took to the South."

Charity was grateful not to have to talk, knowing that Joshua was deliberately not saying anything that required an answer. Certainly he knew she wasn't going to join him in talking about North and South. Too soon, she saw the log cabin set under trees against the base of the mountain that Joshua had described to her, on their way over, as Aunt Nell Morgan's home.

It was a stretched-out cabin with an obviously new addition bumped up against the left side of the original and a wide stone chimney at each end. Smoke drifting out each of them made a soft welcome against the trees.

There were people in front of it, three of them. One was wearing a blue uniform. And the tall, wide woman who must be Aunt Nell was hugging that uniform like it was wrapped around a long lost friend.

Almost without her mind's direction, Charity's legs scrambled to climb over the side of the wagon, even though it was still gently rolling.

"No. I won't stay near any Yankee. I'll just go back."

Joshua reached out a long arm and caught her, pushing her down against the seat a little harder than necessary.

"We talked about it. Men from this valley fought on both sides, Charity. But when they come back and take their uniforms off, they'll be wearing the same kind of clothes again. A year from now you won't be able to tell who fought on which side, except by how they feel toward each other. We have a bigger fight now to get neighbors back to being neighbors again. And you have to help. You knew you're going to be teaching children of both Union and Confederate here. You said you could do it."

"I know. But I wasn't looking at that blue uniform when I said that."

"I don't recognize the soldier, but it might be Willie Bowers. He left to join the army before I knew the people here. He must just have come in to still be wearing that uniform. I'm thinking he'll get out of it as soon as he can. He'll be your closest neighbor here. If it is him, his parents' prayers are answered. Can't you be happy for them, Charity?"

"I prayed, too, Pastor. Daniel didn't come home."

"There are still soldiers coming home all over the South, Charity. We won't give up yet. But I think Nell and Doc have seen us." He pulled the horses to a complete stop.

It was true. The woman had let loose of the soldier and her heavy shoes were pushing against the skirt of her baggy homespun dress, hurrying her over to meet them while the man stayed behind with the soldier.

"Well, it's a great day. Two of our wanderers have come home. Come on down, Charity, and let me get a good look at you. I can tell from here that you look just like your beautiful mama did when she was eighteen. I always told my brother that marrying her was the smartest thing he ever did."

All the time she was talking, she was reaching up to Charity's hand, as though her first thought in any situation was to offer help. Meanwhile, Joshua had climbed down and come over to offer his own help in getting her down from the wagon seat.

Ignoring both of them, Charity flung her wide skirt across the side of the wagon, turned her back on them, and climbed down by herself. Better let them know at the beginning that Charity Charlotte Morgan was going to be beholden to no one.

She turned around to look directly into the mirror image of her own bright blue eyes, looking like the gray-haired woman behind them was struggling not to laugh.

"You're a real Morgan, Charity Charlotte. We'll get along just fine. Am I allowed to hug you?"

Without waiting for permission, she pulled Charity into her arms. Charity started to hug her back, then remembered that those arms had just been hugging that blue uniform. Still, she couldn't turn away from the warmth of her aunt Nell. For the first time in the torment of the last few months, she felt a desire to lay her head on someone's broad shoulder and cry. She shook herself away from such ideas and stood back.

She recited the words she had been mentally practicing all the way across Tennessee and into North Carolina. "Thank you for giving me a home."

"Child, you're going to just make our home better and you're surely a godsend to the valley. We've been worrying at God to send us someone to get the school open again. . .as well as the church. And He's done both in His usual perfect way. But come on now and let me show you your room. You'll be sharing with Bethany till she and Pastor Joshua get through that wedding we're all working on, but it's a big room, thanks to Willie's dad. He built it on, you know. You're going to take some time to rest and get over that trip before you even tell me about it. One thing, though, you've got to meet my husband." A sheen of gentle radiance slipped over her face at the word. "And our neighbor, Willie, just walked in today."

Charity stiffened. But when they turned to walk toward the men, only the doctor and pastor stood there. The man in the blue uniform was gone.

two

Willie Bowers tried to hide the feeling of antagonism toward the man who stood before him in Doc Andrews's front yard, holding out a friendly hand. He knew a little bit about this Pastor Holt—that he had been a circuit rider who preached against the war, but not against either side, and who had been physically hurt more than once for his beliefs.

But not hurt like the soldiers who had gone out to fight for what they believed. This Pastor Holt, who had already said, "Call me Joshua," had stayed away from all that. It was almost as if Willie's body, rather than his mind, had decided to turn away from the outstretched hand, letting his own hang by his side, ignoring the pained look on Doc Andrews's face.

He didn't look at Pastor Holt's face to see if he resented being slighted, but the minister's voice didn't change as he invited Willie to the church services on the coming Sunday. Willie thought that he might decline that invitation, too.

"I'm going to get out of this uniform and help Pa in the field," he said to no one in particular. He turned and walked away, refusing to think about the quick words of consolation that Nell would give to Pastor Holt when she came back from welcoming that redheaded girl in the wagon. But he knew that Nell would be too realistic to try to pretend away his anger, and somehow that made him feel more able to deal with it.

He skirted around the homeplace that Pa had kept adding to until now it stretched straight across the bottom of the mountain like a stopped train. It reminded Willie of the barren freight cars that had carried him and his fellow soldiers across the South to fight and kill men who might have been cousins. Some of the house was log; the latest additions were of unweathered boards.

Behind the house, Falling Water Creek came off the mountain, accepted the waters of a smaller, unnamed stream, and widened before it curved to follow the contours of the valley. Early on, Pa had built a sawmill over the stream, using the moving water to turn a mill wheel and run a saw through felled tree trunks to make boards.

Will smiled, remembering watching his father's skilled hands work with the wood and, when he grew older, helping him. Even when he was a child he had helped by sweeping the sawdust off the floor.

"It seemed like your pa had to keep his hands doing something to keep his mind from running crazy," Mama had told him as part of her happy babbling when he walked in this morning. His father had just held onto his hand and not said anything at all.

Mama had finally sent him off to see Nell and Doc while she dug out his old dungarees so he could get out of his uniform one last time. She'd be fixing a meal like he'd dreamed of over and over nights when he was trying to sleep, cold and hungry. They still didn't have a lot here in the valley, but Pa had had a summer to raise crops without the army or outliers confiscating it, and Mama would find a chicken somewhere that she could get along without.

He was right. Mama was in the kitchen with the yeasty odor of rising bread and a plucked chicken rapidly being turned into breasts and legs under her hands.

When Willie walked in, she put her knife down and ran to him as though she hadn't welcomed him already, earlier in the day.

"Now, you just get that old uniform off and into. . .I got out a set of your pa's clothes. . .you can't get into those you left when you went off to the North. . .my, you've growed six inches. . .I always knew you'd be tall like your pa. . .but, I was afraid. . ."

She let the rest of the sentence slide away while she alternately hugged him and ran her hands over his now broad shoulders. "You walked all night so you could get here this morning. You've been walking for days. Sleep now while I cook this mess of turnips and potatoes. I'll have everything ready when you wake up. Willie, where did you start walking from?" As though he hadn't already told her and his father.

"From Frankfort, over in Kentucky, Mama," he answered patiently. "They took us down to there on a train. We were out in Texas and they wandered us around awhile before they'd let us leave." He hesitated, then determined to speak. "Mama? Do you think you could call me Will instead of Willie? That's what the men I served with called me after. . . well, I did some things in a battle around Stones River in Tennessee, and they said I wasn't a kid anymore and changed my name. I'm more used to Will now. . . ."

"We can do that without ever asking what you did. . . Will." Pa had come into the kitchen and stood behind them. Though he didn't touch his son, when they turned to him, his eyes held a quiet pride and happiness, and his look at his wife told her not to argue.

"I'll try to remember, Samuel," she said, her face showing the tears she was trying to hold back. "Now, just you go along and rest and get out of that uniform." Her voice put heavy lines under every word. "I'm going to throw it away," she muttered, turning back to the chicken.

"No, Annie," Pa said in a firm voice, "we're going to keep that uniform to remind ourselves of how our son fought to keep the Union together."

She didn't answer, concentrating on a thigh joint that seemed to be particularly stubborn against her knife.

Will went into his old room and put on his father's dungarees and homespun shirt, reveling in the softness of them. Then, instead of resting as Mama wanted, he went outside with his father to look over the fields of corn and oats. The feel of the wet soil was good to Will's hands. Even the tiny rocks of the grubbed-out fields looked good to him.

When they came in, Mama had covered the table in her kitchen with the cloth her mother had woven, only brought out for special occasions. The faint scent of the lavender sprigs kept in its folds nestled under the broader smells of steamy food.

The fried chicken, potatoes and turnips creamed together, green beans, and raised rolls made him think again of how many times he'd longed for his mother's cooking, and he pleased them both by the way he ate.

But he still didn't feel like he needed rest.

"I'm going up on the mountain awhile before it gets dark, Mama. I'll rest tonight."

He shook his thoughts off as he headed toward the mountain. He didn't want to remember anything now. He just wanted to absorb the color, the mist, the feel of these mountains that were like no other place he'd been in the years he'd been gone. It didn't matter that he'd been through other mountains, some bigger than these. They weren't these mountains, and he'd never stopped waking up every morning longing for them.

Now he was thinking of those hidden places, known only to himself, where he had played in what seemed like another world of childhood only dimly remembered. He came into one of his retreats where no trees grew, though they surrounded it. As a child he had thought of it as a bowl like the crocks in his mother's kitchen. Now he stopped and let his gaze take in the familiar cove. Several bright scarlet sumacs grew near the edges of the trees, and patches of dandelion and clover crowded the grass.

He sat on a large stone and allowed himself to relax. Already he felt better, more like the old Willie Bowers, though he would insist on being called Will now. He even let himself feel a moment of remorse for walking away without shaking the preacher's hand earlier. Maybe he'd find him sometime and apologize. Maybe not. He didn't have to do anything now. Not one thing. He didn't have to get up when someone said, or go over any hill into gunfire, or ram shot into his own gun, or taste powder in his mouth, or shoot. . .

He stopped himself. He'd not come out here to remember battles. He started thinking of things he could do now—wear whatever clothes were there when he got up in the morning, sleep on a fresh-smelling corn shuck bed with maybe even a feather ticking, go hunting, which was what a man should do with guns. He thought of the brass-fitted, European-made shotgun he'd bought off a soldier on the edge of Knoxville and carried home. He could easily bring deer and turkey meat home to help his family through the winter. Later, though, after he got back his mountain man feeling about guns.

A sudden movement near the trees got his attention. But he didn't find himself wishing for his gun as he might have before the war. Even if it should be a deer or a bear, it was part of his mountains, and he just wanted to sit still and watch it.

He only realized that it was a person when he saw skirts flashing across his retreat, running away from him.

"Wait," he called, jumping up instinctively. The girl only ran faster, about to disappear into the trees.

"Wait," he called again. "Wait. I won't hurt you. I just want to see who you are. I don't remember you from when I lived here."

She turned and grimaced at him as he bore down on her. "I know who you are. . .Yankee." The word seemed to explode from her stretched mouth.

Will stopped so quickly he almost tripped himself. "You're the girl that Miss Nell and Doc took in."

She stood up straighter. "I'm not a girl anybody took in. I'm the new schoolteacher."

"Well, you sure don't act like a schoolteacher. Running away from me like a little kid. What are you doing out here, anyway? Did you run away from Miss Nell, too? She'd never let you wander off not knowing the mountain." He put his hand on her arm. "You're lost, aren't you?"

She jerked away. "No, I'm certainly not lost and I didn't run away. I left while Aunt Nell and Uncle Doc went out to see about someone sick and I haven't seen Bethany yet. I'm not really lost. I can get back by myself."

He walked over and sat back down on his rock. "All right. Which way are you going to go to get back by yourself?"

Charity frowned at him. She had the uncomfortable feeling that he might be laughing at her and she didn't like it. She decided that she wouldn't have liked him even if he wasn't a Yankee, even if he was undoubtedly the handsomest man she'd ever seen with his brown hair brushing against his collarless shirt and his long legs making even those near shapeless pants look almost elegant. He could have been leaning back in a velvet chair in some ladies' parlor in Nashville, the way he sat on that rock. But something in his strong face told her he would never choose a velvet chair.

She thought for a minute about his question. Her innate common sense told her that she had been foolish to wander off alone. She had meant to stay on the main road in the valley, but the mountain intrigued her and she promised herself she would go only a little way up, just to prove to herself—or to the mountain—that she wasn't afraid of it. She had carefully chosen landmarks, but trees and rocks seemed to copy each other in this wilderness, and she didn't remember how she had happened onto this little cove. And the near evening breeze was getting chilly. But was she going to admit all that to this provoking face?

"Why, down, of course," she said, triumphantly.

He grinned. "Of course. Which way is down? We're on a shoulder now. You could walk a pretty good way without going either up or down."

She threw her own shoulders back and met his gaze defiantly. "All right. I'm lost."

He waited for more, then realized she wasn't going to ask him for help. Even lost, she still was being stubbornly independent. Well, he couldn't leave her here. Didn't want to, he admitted to himself.

He stood up. "Come on. I'll take you home." Then he couldn't resist a comment. "That is, if you don't mind following a Yankee."

She didn't answer, just waited for him to go ahead of her. All the way down the mountain, he heard her following behind him. He didn't slow down for her or try to pressure her by going fast. It was a short way down, much shorter than she had probably thought it was in the panic that she must have felt.

"It's all right now. There's Birdsong Road." Her voice was small, words coming between puffs.

"Birdsong Road?"

"I call it that."

"Why?"

"Because I want to."

He let that go. "Do you know which way to go to get home?"

"Of course. That way."

"Then I'll go back the way we came."

She was angling toward the road, her feet shuffling through leaves. "It wasn't so far down," she threw over her shoulder. "I would have found the way." She walked a few steps farther, then stopped. "But thank you," she said, without turning. Then she walked on.

He strode back up, making his own way above her so that he kept her in sight until she reached home. It was getting too close to dark to let her be out alone in this place that was still strange to her. And, he admitted, he enjoyed watching her. She was a sight with those blue eyes and that red hair. She was, for sure.

three

When Charity reached home, she found her aunt Nell and uncle Doc waiting anxiously for her in front of the cabin.

Aunt Nell folded her into her arms. "We were worried about you." Her voice held only a mild reproach. "You shouldn't wander off alone yet. Bears are out getting fat for the winter and there's other things. . .some people. . .that can. . .that might. . .hurt you. Doc or Bethany or I'll take you out till you learn your way around. Anyway, I'm glad you didn't get lost."

Charity found it easy to return her hug, but she didn't think it was worthwhile to explain about getting lost. . . and found. She didn't want to talk about that Yankee.

Uncle Doc, not as demonstrative as Aunt Nell, put one hand on each of their shoulders, and Charity noticed that they were all the same height. She thought that a breadboard set across their heads would be perfectly level.

"Come on in now and meet my daughter. She's working up something for our supper. And it's about to get dark," Uncle Doc said.

Charity looked up at the encircling mountains, feeling a jolt of something close to fear as shadows of dusk darkened their colors and turned them into threatening giants looming over her on all sides. For a moment she felt the overwhelming presence that must have made primitive people try to ward off their menace with worship. Then her basic knowledge of God pushed the emotion away. But would she ever learn to love these mountains as Pastor Joshua had suggested she would?

It was with a feeling of relief that she followed Aunt Nell and Uncle Doc across the porch that stretched along the front of the house to a door that the new addition had made a bit off center. Another door to the right led to the room Aunt Nell had briefly explained earlier was the bedroom and workroom she and Uncle Doc shared. They had evidently decided that the new addition didn't need an outside door, though the porch had been extended in front of it.

As she accepted the safety of the door closing behind her, shutting out the mountains, Charity admitted a grudging thankfulness to Will Bowers for keeping her from wandering lost up there in those threatening hulks.

Inside, a slender young woman with brown hair pulled up in a bun moved about the kitchen end of a huge room. Charity had stayed in the room only briefly after Uncle Doc and Aunt Nell had gone away, apologizing for leaving so soon to treat someone who had been caught under a falling tree. Something inside her had pushed her out of the house; something that was like running away without knowing a place to run to.

She looked at the room more deeply now. A wide table with several chairs sat before the window on one side, and a long narrow one covered with jars and sacks was across from it. Charity guessed that it was used as a work table of some kind. The rest of the room was sparsely furnished with chairs and two chairside tables, one of which looked even from this distance to be of superior workmanship. At the far end of the room, a narrow bed was covered with a colorful blanket. Charity wondered who used it, since she had already seen the built-on room where she and Bethany, who must be this woman, would be sleeping till Bethany and Joshua Holt got married.

She was pulled back from her survey of the room by Uncle Doc's proud voice. "This is my daughter, Bethany. Nell and I hope you two will be friends."

Bethany turned from the good smelling pot she was stirring and hurried over to hug Charity. "I've been feeling like we're friends ever since Joshua left to bring you in here."

Charity let the thought run through her mind that she hadn't had so many hugs since that time eons ago when she lived with her family back in Williamson County, before the war killed everyone. She felt tears somewhere behind her eyes as she realized how much she had missed the human touch.

She forced herself not to turn away to hide her emotion. "Thank you for letting him go after me," she said.

Bethany laughed. "Oh, I hardly missed him. He's spending so much time working on the church and trying to talk people into getting together enough to come to meetings, I don't see him except when I'm working with him."

"Which is most of the time." Nell looked affectionately at her stepdaughter. "The rest of the time, she's working on her wedding dress."

Bethany laughed again as she stepped back to the fireplace. "Well, it's getting close to the day we've set and I still have a little work to do on the dress. But I'm going to spend some time helping you get the school opened, too."

She gave the pot a quick stir and slipped a long-handled spatula under a corn pone near the edge of the fireplace. Though a tiny black iron stove stood beside the large fireplace, she didn't seem to be using it.

"It's ready, I think. It's all the things we pulled out of the garden last week, potatoes and turnips and carrots and such. No meat, I'm afraid. No one has paid us in meat this week."

"They're saying, 'Wait till we butcher that pig'," Doc said, smiling easily. "But they still have so few animals it hurts me to take their meat."

Bethany settled them at the table, Doc and Nell at each end, before she dished up the stew and sat beside Charity. For a few minutes after the blessing, there was silence as they concentrated on enjoying the food. The oniony vegetables were delicious and the hot bread was so good, Charity almost wanted to hold it in her mouth instead of swallowing it.

After a bit, Doc turned to Charity.

"What do you want to do tomorrow, Charity?"

"Rest," said Nell and Bethany together.

"No, I think I want to go down and see the school," Charity decided.

Doc nodded approvingly. "Good girl. The sooner we see what needs to be done there, the sooner we can get it open. We need to get these children in while the crops are harvested and before the snows hit."

"Snows?"

"Sometimes we're buried in snow. Some winters we hardly have any. But it gets cold in these mountains and I'm afraid too many parents put getting wood cut before getting their sons to learn to read and write."

"And daughters, Dad. We're going to bring in the girls, too." Bethany looked determined.

"I don't object to that, but a lot of mothers will. Especially if those daughters have little brothers and sisters to be cared for."

"Am I going to teach them together? Boys and girls?" Charity thought of the school in Miss Jane Curtis's parlor at the edge of Nashville, where she and a few other daughters of well-to-do plantation owners had been driven in buggies to learn reading and writing along with manners and embroidery. And where she had helped teach the new ones when she grew older.

She admitted to herself that trying to teach in that little building she had seen near the mouth of the valley scared her. Now she knew that she would not only be teaching boys and girls together, she would be teaching children who may have picked up their parents' anger toward each other.

Aunt Nell looked at her with understanding. "It will be all right, Charity Charlotte Morgan," she said. "You can do whatever needs to be done. But now you need to just get a good night's sleep. Bethany, I'll wash up. You and Charity may want to decide who's going to store what where in your room." She let the muddled sentence stand.

"I could sleep in that bed," Charity pointed at the colorful bed at the end of the room, "and not bother Bethany."

"You'll be a pleasure, not a bother," Bethany assured her. "Sometimes when Dad or Nell come in late from a patient, they sleep there so as not to wake the other one in their room. And Nell keeps her herbs in here." She pointed toward the sacks and jars on the table against the other wall. "She works in here pretty late lots of nights."

In the room Charity discovered that Joshua and Bethany had moved in the little bit that she had been able to rescue from her home. They had created a small retreat in one end of the room. She ran her hands over the gilt design on the back of the Boston rocker and touched the pitcher and basin that sat on the small chest by her bed. The screen covered with bluebirds sitting on stylized trees, which they had set up to give her privacy, took her back to her bedroom in Williamson County.

"This is the closest I've been to being home since Mama died," she whispered to herself just before drifting off into an exhausted sleep.

four

"It shouldn't be in too bad condition," Bethany said. "We used it sometimes when bushwhackers came through the valley during the war. . .if someone got hurt, we treated them here."

Charity looked at her in admiration. Bethany seemed to be capable of accepting the wrongs of the war without anger or blame. But, then, she hadn't lost her mother from a heart attack brought on by soldiers occupying their home and she hadn't lost her brother somewhere in the war. She must have lost her mother sometime, though, since her father was married to Aunt Nell. Charity decided there was much to learn about these people who lived in the valley.

She and Bethany and Aunt Nell were walking up the path to the school from Birdsong Road. The morning was bright with sunshine beaming that wonderful color through the sugar maples. Only a few patches lingered on the mountaintops.

Bethany and Aunt Nell had rushed her through breakfast to come down to the school. Charity had a strong sense that they were more enthusiastic about her opening the school than she was. Still, she was beginning to catch some of their enthusiasm herself. Immersion in the school might help put her mental ghosts to rest.

The door to the log building was closed and didn't give to their pushes. "Is it locked, Nell?" Bethany asked.

"There's no sign of a lock on this door. Never has been," Nell answered. "Either there's something blocking it inside or it's just stuck. The hinges may need tightening up. It gets draggy as the building settles. Let's all push together."

After a bit of jockeying to get all three shoulders ready to hit the door at once, they drew back and pushed at Aunt Nell's "now." The door burst open and they staggered in, clutching each other to keep from falling. Laughing helplessly, they turned it into a hug. Charity felt the same faint stir of thankfulness that she had found a place for herself here among this loving family that she had felt the night before.

Slowly, they separated themselves and looked around. A wide aisle down the center separated two short rows of sturdy wooden benches with low backs.

"Good," Charity murmured almost to herself. "I can separate the boys and girls." She tried not to compare the unpainted benches with the scrolled, ball-footed, straight chairs she and two or three other girls sat on in Miss Jane's parlor. This schoolroom looked like an infinitely greater challenge than assisting Miss Jane. But she liked a challenge. She determined that she would make this project take her away from the sorrowful thoughts that so often filled her mind now.

"The first challenge is to get a lot of good soapy water," she said aloud, not thinking that the other two might not be following her train of thought.

Whether they were or not, they quickly agreed with her. "I see a few cobwebs around, too," Aunt Nell said. "Well, more than a few. You can see them really well there where the sun is coming in."

"I'm glad there are two windows on each side," Charity said. "We'll have plenty of light."

"But, speaking of cleaning, I've promised to help some of the women wash in the church today." Bethany moved toward the door.

"And I need to check on Lizzie Williams. That baby's about ready to come. Charity, if you'd like to go back to the house with us and get a good rest today, we'll bring buckets and rags down in a few days."

"Thanks," Charity said, "but I see a broom there. I think I'll sweep out and maybe get some of those spider webs down." The thought of staying around the cabin with nothing to do didn't seem like rest to her. Briskly pushing a broom over the schoolroom floor and walls would be better.

Aunt Nell seemed to understand. "You should be safe here. Sometimes the hotheads here in the valley seem about to shoot each other, but they won't hurt the new schoolmarm."

"You won't get lost going home?" Bethany asked.

Charity felt a grin coming on her face. "How could I get lost? Birdsong Road goes straight up the middle of the valley."

Bethany smiled back. "You've already given the valley something. We've never thought to name the road, and you've brought us a beautiful name. I like it. It's a pretty long road, though, and walking back will be too tiring for you. I'll get Rainbow—that's my horse—she's easy to ride—down to you. You'll like her."

Charity didn't like to refuse Bethany's offer after refusing their suggestions for resting, so she smiled and nodded her head. She hadn't seen their horses yet, but she had ridden all her life, and any horse named Rainbow had to be easy to ride.

When they were gone, she grabbed up the broom. She had dug several angry spiders, who had settled in for the winter, out of their corners and was vigorously chasing them down for the kill when she heard a horse being reined in outside.

Expecting Bethany to leave Rainbow and go back to the church, she didn't go to the door. She was punching away at an unusually large spider in the corner behind the rough table she was going to use for a desk when she became aware of someone standing in the doorway.

"I can see that Ira Krantz is going to be kept busy making brooms for you if you're going to use them like that," a masculine voice said. "Can I help you attack whatever it is you have cornered there?"

A voice she recognized. The Yankee. She whirled around.

"I don't need any help attacking from a Yankee."

Will Bowers strode past the benches, his heavy shoes hitting the floor with a sound that made her think of armies clashing. He stopped directly in front of her.

"You can stop that Yankee calling." His words were coming spaced out from low in his throat. "I'm a Southerner just as much as you are. I was born here and I grew up in this valley. Just because I fought to keep our country together, it doesn't make me anything different."

She faced him, refusing to look down from the blaze in his eyes. "It makes you in the army that burned down my house. And that after we'd let them use it for a headquarters."

"Listen, Childish Charity, I'm truly sorry about what

happened to you, but there was bad and good on both sides and altogether it was ugly. Still is, with men riding around the main roads killing and beating each other. But I'm back where I want to be now and nobody is going to chase me away. I'm a Southerner and I'm a valley man and I mean to stay."

She jerked the broom up and slammed the bristles against the corner. "Don't call me Childish Charity."

"If I can stand thinking about your name. . ." He didn't finish the sentence.

She turned in surprise, letting the broom drop to the floor. "Charity? What's wrong with Charity?"

"Not Charity. Your last name. You don't know about Morgan? That Rebel spy? Everyone in my company did. Everyone still alive after the ambush anyway. Most of them were wiped out. . .they were all around me. . .dead or wishing they were dead. Later we found out it was Morgan told the Rebs where we'd be marching. That's the only name we knew him by, and we all cheered when someone rode in and said he'd heard Morgan was killed. I hope he was. Any one of us could have killed him ourselves."

"Well, I don't know any Morgan who was a spy. My brother fought for the South and he's dead now or I'd have heard from him." She felt sudden tears bubbling out of her eyes and tried to turn away to hide them, but Will's hands on her shoulders stopped her.

"I'm sorry," he said, moving one hand to wipe the wetness from her cheeks. "I had no right to talk to you like that. You can't help that someone had the same name as you. I always tried to remember Miss Nell whenever I thought of him and now I'll think of you."

Charity didn't want to listen to him or admit to herself that his touch was comforting or that for a moment she felt herself wanting to get closer to him. She pulled away and turned her back on him, staring into the corner.

"Oh, now you've let that spider get away and it was a wild one. It's gone down into that stuff there."

He didn't move. "That stuff is a mouse nest." He seemed glad to let the conversation change. "It looks like you need some help cleaning out the varmints."

"I don't need any help, thank you. Why did you come?"

"Bethany asked me to bring Rainbow down to you."

She found herself almost angry with him for not sounding like her beaux back home and saying he came just to see her. She was about to coldly ask him to leave when something ran across the floor near the door. For the moment, she forgot her anger. "What was that?"

"A mouse maybe. Sounded big enough to be a rat. Might have been just a squirrel. Yes, you definitely need help clearing out the varmints."

Before she could refuse his help, a strange man came into view in the open door. Charity felt a moment of gratitude for Will's presence, then pushed it down. The man at the door didn't look like someone she would need to fear.

He was dressed rather better than the men she'd seen in the valley, his long legs encased in boots that looked both well worn and well made. Tightly woven pants that reminded her of clothes worn by her friends in Williamson County were tucked into the boots and topped by an open-collared gray shirt. He carried a black-brimmed hat in his left hand.

With a curt nod to Will, he turned brown eyes in slightly

narrowed lids on her. "So this is the new schoolmarm. I hoped when I passed by and saw the door open that I could meet you and offer you any help I can. Dave Bradley, ma'am." He dipped his head toward her, then nodded again to Will. "I heard you were back, Willie."

"Will, please." Will didn't offer his hand, nor did the newcomer.

"Will, now?" His lips twitched slightly.

Will didn't pretend a smile. He looked somewhere near angry, and Charity found herself in turn almost enjoying his anger, without forcing herself to analyze the emotion.

Dave Bradley smiled at her and she returned it easily.

"Remember," he said with a nod and a two-handed gesture that made her feel drawn into a circle that left Will Bowers out, "anything I can do to help, ma'am, just let me know." Without another look at Will, he turned and went out.

Charity turned her amused attention to Will. "You don't like him. I bet he's a good Southerner."

"I'm a good Southerner. I don't know if he fought North or South. Nobody does. He's a man who won't hold up out loud for whatever he believes. I don't care beans about him. I'll help you get this door closed. It sticks sometimes."

"No. I've started to sweep the floor and I'm going to finish."

"Then I'll wait for you," he said stubbornly, putting one brogan up on a back bench. "I can't believe that Bethany and Miss Nell left you here alone. Anybody can come in. Promise me you won't come down here alone again."

"I won't promise you anything. I'll come down here whenever I want."

He glared at her for a moment, then sighed, seeming to admit her stubbornness. "Then I'm going to leave my shotgun here. Can you shoot?"

"Of course, I can. My brother taught me before he left. But I don't need your gun around." It was true that Daniel had showed her how to safely load and shoot a gun, but she had never felt at ease with one.

He ignored that. "This gun was made in Europe. You can tell by all the brass fittings. Have you ever used a shotgun?"

She drew herself up to be as tall as possible. "I can shoot any gun. But I couldn't shoot a man."

He winced. "Mostly people do what they have to. But there's others than men, animals come down off the mountains." He went out without saying any more and returned with the gun.

"It's loaded. The hammer's half cocked. You have to pull it back one more time, aim, and pull the trigger. You don't even have to aim very true because the shot scatters out. I'm hiding it here between these logs. Please don't tell anyone it's here. I don't want to lose it."

"I wish you wouldn't leave it. You don't have to leave it."

"But I will. Unless you agree to let me come down with you."

"I won't."

He didn't answer, but slid his gun between the lowest log and the floor. Charity looked at him in surprise. He was really leaving his gun for her. A modern gun like that must be dear to him. Why was he willing to take a chance on losing it just to protect her? She almost bent and agreed to let him come down to the school with her. But she wasn't going to agree to tell someone like him every time she wanted to come to the school.

She turned back to her sweeping. "You really don't have to stay."

"I know, but I am."

Seeing his determined face, Charity gave in. She wasn't about to continue sweeping with his calm eyes following her every move.

"I guess I'll wait till later."

She replaced the broom and walked out the door without waiting to see if it stuck.

The untethered mare that Bethany had called Rainbow was walking slowly across the schoolyard, her head down, as she looked for grass to nibble. At a sound made by Will, she raised her head and came to stand by a cut stump.

Will moved to help her, but Charity, thankful for her long legs, stepped up on the stump and into the saddle without appearing to notice his gesture. Determined to leave him behind, she gave Rainbow a sharp slap on the flank. The surprised Rainbow jumped forward and dashed down the short lane to Birdsong Road. Her left foot slipped slightly on a pile of wet leaves, but she recovered, and Charity, a good and experienced rider, kept her seat.

Enjoying riding a running horse again, Charity kept Rainbow at the closest the little horse could get to a gallop until she was well up the road away from Will's sight.

She was carefully rubbing Rainbow down in the stable behind their cabin when Will came in, his rapid breathing making Charity think that he had used his army quick step to follow them.

His eyes were furious. "Don't you dare hit Bethany's horse ever again," he said, without any greeting. "Bethany never does that. And she wouldn't make Rainbow run unless she just had to get to someone who needed her. Rainbow could have broken a leg when she slipped on those leaves." He ran his hand over Rainbow's back. "Did you rub her down good?"

"Will Bowers, I know how to take care of a horse and I don't need—a—" Something in his eyes told her not to call him Yankee again. "You to check on me."

With a glance into Rainbow's feed box to be sure there were oats there, she flounced out and walked to the house, not looking back, though some instinct told her that he had followed her out and stood watching her go.

five

"Perhaps you'd like to see the church today, Charity. We're cleaning again, and it would be a good time for you to meet some of the women. And maybe set a day for us all to come down and help you clean the school. The women, at least the ones who helped us open the church, are anxious to get the school open, too."

"Bethany, you keep talking about opening the church. Hasn't there been one here before?"

"Oh, the church building has been here since the valley was settled, but it was closed during the war."

"Why? Our church back in Williamson County stayed open. They had battles all around and the Yankees were there, but nobody made us close the church, except after a battle sometimes, when it was being used for a hospital."

"Nobody made us close the church here, either. Well, no army came in and said we had to close it, but bushwhackers beat up the preacher we had then, and he. . .well, he didn't have much grit. . .he sneaked out of the valley one night and we never heard any more from him. We could have had services with men of the neighborhood, but the people who live here were, actually still are, so divided between Union and Confederate that there weren't enough of one mind to make the effort to open it again. Not a lot of them will come to services now, but Joshua is determined to make it a part of the community again."

"I know. The church and marrying you were about all he talked about on our trip over."

Bethany smiled, a soft shine appearing in her eyes. "Joshua and I have waited. . . Having him here in the valley to stay is an answer to prayer."

Charity forced herself not to turn away from the happiness in the other woman's eyes. She couldn't believe that she would ever feel really happy again. "I'd love to come with you to the church," she said.

The church, like the school, was set back down a short lane from Birdsong Road. The rough gray stones in the cemetery and the old wooden church with its two doors looked like they had been there always.

"Why two doors?" she asked Bethany. "It's such a small building."

"It's an old-fashioned idea, but one is for men and one for women. Then they sit that way inside, too."

"Families don't sit together?"

"No. The children sit with the mother till the boys get old enough to move to the men's side. Joshua and I have joked that we should designate one door for Confederates and one for Union. There might be fewer fights in church." In spite of saying it was a joke, Bethany sounded wistful.

Inside, it looked the same as the school, with long benches on each side of a center aisle. In contrast to the school, though, it looked clean and smelled of soap.

"I don't see any spiders," Charity murmured.

Bethany laughed. "We convinced them that spiders don't need to go to church," she said. "Using brooms, I'm afraid. Spiders don't answer much to words." •

Charity laughed with her, then they both turned as

three women in the usual loose homespun dresses came into the church through the door that Bethany had identified as the men's entrance. Charity found herself wondering if it was some sort of secret rebellion against the designation before she realized that they had stopped at the door to stare at her in friendly curiosity.

Bethany took her hand and led her toward the women. "Charity Charlotte Morgan, this is Tabitha Ballard, Virgie Smith, and Annie Bowers. They helped us get the church cleaned. Annie is Will's mother," she added, unnecessarily.

"And now we're cleaning it down to the last bit of dust for a wedding," the taller one called Tabitha said. "We'll help you with the school, too, Charity Charlotte Morgan. We're just powerful glad to have Nell Morgan's niece come in to teach our children."

Virgie Smith nodded vigorously. "Glad to make your acquaintance, Charity Charlotte," she said.

Charity tried to hide a panicky feeling that Virgie and Tabitha were dressed so much alike in loose gray homespun with apron to match and wore their hair so much alike in low buns that she might not remember which was which. She noticed that Tabitha's eyes were on a level with hers and she looked down at Virgie. "Tall Tabitha," she said to herself, noting that Tabitha was also somewhat broader than Virgie. She knew she wouldn't have any trouble remembering Annie Bowers, who was quietly beaming at her.

"Let's set a day right now to give that schoolhouse a good cleaning," Virgie said. "Let's see. This is Wednesday and we're about through here and the wedding comes next. We'll have time to work at the school. How about Friday?"

They agreed on Friday. Charity thanked them and told

them she was going on down to the school. "I think all the spiders you refused religion to have gone down to get an education," she explained to the amused women.

"Just keep the door closed so nobody knows you're in there alone," Tabitha said. "I already know from your aunt Nell that there's no point in telling anybody in your family not to wander around alone. She's been riding alone in this valley for near forty years. Getting married to Doc hasn't changed her much."

Bethany smiled. "At least she usually only goes out for births now. Dad takes care of most of the sickness."

"And we don't forget that you still help out some, Bethany."

"Not so much since Dad's back from the war. But I do like helping with the children. I like to comfort them." She turned to Charity, holding out a bucket. "You can take this. We won't be using it today. Now, don't stay long or try to do much. Remember you'll have help later."

As Charity went out, she heard them continuing the conversation, one of the women commenting on how lucky the valley was to have people with medical knowledge living there.

She hurried out to the road and down to the school, not meeting anyone on the way.

The door must have been limbered up some by the coming and going of the day before for it opened easily to her push. She went immediately to pick up the heavy-handled broom, determined to get the spiders out.

A soft slither of movement over beside a bench caught her attention. A mouse? Please, not a rat. The sound stopped. Maybe she'd imagined it. Slowly, carrying the broom with handle out like a weapon, she tiptoed toward the bench.

She was looking at the black body of a snake, a body that seemed to go on and on. Heart in her mouth, she froze, surprised to find herself wishing for Joshua, Dave, even Will. . .anyone with strong muscles and no fear of snakes. Snakes made her weak.

But there was no one here but her. No wonder Will had left her a gun. It wasn't just a man he'd been thinking of. She'd known that she couldn't shoot a man. . .but a snake was different.

The shiny body lay still, only the head lifted. Was it watching her? Trying to decide where to bite? Trying to hypnotize her? Slowly, she backed away to where Will had hidden the gun. Keeping her eyes focused on the snake's barely moving head, she bent her knees enough to reach behind her for the gun. She felt the metal beneath one palm and closed her hand around it, pulling against it—and found she couldn't lift it with one hand. Will hadn't told her it was so heavy, and when her brother had taught her to fire, he'd handed the gun to her. There was nothing to do but turn her back on the snake and hope that it wouldn't take the chance to sneak up on her.

"Don't be silly, Charity Charlotte Morgan," she said out loud. "It's a snake. It can't think."

She forced herself to turn and pick up the gun with both hands, then turned back again. The snake hadn't moved. Maybe it thought it was hiding. Slowly, she brought the gun up, stretched out her arm to press the smooth stock against her shoulder, and pulled back the hammer like Will had said. She managed to find the thumblike head between the wide sights, glad that she didn't have to hold the heavy barrel level with her outstretched and shaking left arm.

She wrapped her finger around the trigger and pressed it. An explosion of sound, bits of snake and pieces of wood scattering into the air, and a surprising slam against her shoulder all seemed to happen at once.

It took Charity several breaths to recognize the hard surface under her stretched-out legs as the floor, while her shaking hands let the gun clatter down beside her.

As soon as she could move, Charity left the gun on the floor and staggered outside, trying not to see pieces of snake dripping from the wall and on the floor. She leaned against the logs of the building, letting her arm swing down, then up across her chest. Her shoulder might never belong to her again. She tried to force her breathing into some semblance of regularity, while waiting for her heart to get itself back into her chest.

"All right, Charity, it's in there and if you don't want to find it tomorrow, you've got to go in and sweep it out now. Look at me, I'm talking to myself, but don't I have a reason to?"

She pulled away from the wall and forced herself back into the schoolhouse. Without looking at the snake, she grabbed the bucket and took it back to the spring, walking carefully, remembering that people said if you see a snake, watch out for its mate. Every movement of grass, even the sound of her own skirts dragging against the grass, made her heart jump. But she was determined. No one was going to think she couldn't handle a little—no, a big—snake by herself.

Inside the school, she strode to the bench and pitched her bucket of water over the wall and bench, then swept everything across the bare boards and out the door. What looked like most of the snake still stretched across the floor. She pushed it with the broom, but it was too heavy to move. She left it there, deciding to think about it for a while before she picked it up to throw away. Maybe she could hook it over the end of the broom handle and fling it out. She moved to the door again, needing more fresh air.

Will Bowers was just getting down from a horse. *Oh, no, what else am I going to have to put up with today*? He dropped the reins on the ground and came toward her.

"My mother told me last night that you were going to the church today. I didn't think you'd be down here or I wouldn't have. . ." He stopped directly in front of her and touched her shoulder. "But you're trembling and—no! You didn't see the snake?"

"See the snake?"

"You did, didn't you? Just stay out here and I'll get it."

"Get it?"

"To take it home. Pa would be mad at me if anything happened to it."

"Mad at you? Happen to it?"

Feeling like a parrot, she followed him inside while he continued to talk, not seeming to hear her words.

"I brought Pa's blacksnake that he keeps in the corn crib to kill the rats and mice. . ." He stopped, looking at her confused expression. "Blacksnakes do that. . .kill them. . .and I brought it over and put it in here to get rid of your varmints and. . .smells like the war in here. You shoot that gun?" A strange look came over his face as he moved in sight of the motionless black tail by the bench. "At the snake?"

"I. . .didn't. . .didn't know. . .it was looking at me. . .I. . . your dad will be mad at you?"

A grin was tugging at the corners of his mouth and suddenly he gave in to it, leaning against the bench and laughing loud and long. "And I worried about you seeing a mouse or a rat. I suppose you reloaded in case another varmint comes around?"

She shook her head. "I didn't think of it and. . .I don't know how. I was just trying to think of some way to get rid of that. . .thing," she pointed at the snake's body, "without having to pick it up. But will your father really be mad at you. . .or me, I guess?"

He shook his head. "Right now, he wouldn't be mad at me for anything and Mama will shout praises to you. She won't go into the corn crib when the snake's in there. She can't believe that blacksnakes won't hurt her. I'll just have to find Pa another snake before they hibernate."

He picked up the snake, then stood looking at the wet floor. "You gave it a bath before you killed it?"

She shook her head helplessly. "There were pieces. . .all over. . .I washed them away."

"I bet there was pieces all over, with that gun." Suddenly, his face stiffened, all humor gone. "I've seen. . ." He strode out the door and she knew that he would never finish the sentence.

He didn't come back. She stood in the door and watched him fling the snake toward the grass and get on his horse. His expression didn't change from the one he'd let take over when he remembered the war. For the first time, she let herself realize that war had hurt the Union fighters, too.

six

She didn't want to think about any Yankee soldier, especially one that she seemed to be thinking about more than she wanted.

As she stood there, another horse came into the schoolyard. Dave Bradley swung down. It was too late to step back from the door. He came toward her, watching her intently.

"I hoped to find you here," he said. "Aren't the women helping you clean?"

Charity smiled. Somehow she didn't feel the ambivalence that she always felt with Will. "They're going to help later. I'm just going to get rid of some spiders and. . .other varmints." She decided not to tell him about the snake.

"Well, I came by to tell you that I'm going to round up some of the men in the valley and we'll whitewash the inside for you."

"Oh, that would be wonderful," she said. "That will make it so bright and clean looking for the children."

"I'll see to it then. Good day, Miss Charity."

He went back and swung easily onto his horse from the ground. Charity was relieved to see him go. She decided not to do any more work—not that she had actually done any work, she reminded herself.

She started walking up Birdsong Road, glad of the exercise and hoping not to meet anyone before home.

◌

"I hear that we have a great hunter in the family," Uncle Doc said. He and Aunt Nell and Charity were seated at the table enjoying huge bowls of potato soup with corn-bread and milk. Bethany was visiting a neighbor with Pastor Holt.

The barely held-in laughter in Uncle Doc's eyes told Charity that he had heard the story of the snake. So Will Bowers was not only everything she had thought about him before, he was also a tattletale. Probably had exaggerated the story, too. Probably said there were pieces of the snake on the ceiling, hanging out the window. She didn't answer Uncle Doc.

"Looks to me like, whatever you're talking about, it's embarrassing to Charity, and that's not good for her digestion. Can it wait?" Aunt Nell said.

"Of course. Charity, I'm seriously proud to know that you're a good enough shot to hit a snake. That's not always easy." Uncle Doc was still holding back amusement.

"Charity," Aunt Nell looked shocked. "You had to kill a snake? Doc, what are you laughing at? This is serious. It didn't bite you, did it?"

"It wouldn't dare get that close," Uncle Doc said. Now he was laughing outright.

Charity sat up a little straighter. "It was a blacksnake, Aunt Nell."

"Samuel Bowers's favorite blacksnake," Uncle Doc interjected.

"You mean the one that. . .hmm. . .strange man keeps in his corn crib? The one that Annie is so scared of?"

Charity dipped a spoonful of soup, then put it back

without bringing it to her mouth. "I believe it was," she admitted.

"Then you've made one good friend who will be grateful to you for life. Annie hated that snake. But how did you happen to kill it?"

"Will took it to the schoolhouse to kill the mice. He thought I was going to be at the church today."

Aunt Nell chuckled, beginning to see the humor in the story. "And you saw it and killed it. I'm proud of you, Charity. Lots of women would have just run. But I didn't know you had a gun down there."

"Will left his shotgun. He thought that I should have it when I refused to promise not to stay down there alone."

Uncle Doc nodded, a gleam of mischief still in his eye. "He seems to be seriously concerned about your wellbeing. And he was right. You did need the gun. But, I'm proud of you, too, sweetheart."

Bethany came in then. She gave them a tired smile and dipped herself a bowl of soup.

"How did your visits go?" Aunt Nell asked.

Bethany grimaced. "Only fair. Carl Dietz says now that he won't even think about going to any church with Union sympathizers. I think Sophie would go, but she'll do what Carl wants. We hope we can change his mind, at least get him to go in the church, if he won't sit near certain people. He particularly mentioned Willie Bowers. How can anyone hold a grudge against someone who grew up here? Who is one of us? How long is it going to take us to let the war go?"

"Longer than any of us can live, I imagine," Aunt Nell answered seriously.

"But, Charity, what kind of day did you have?" Bethany asked.

Uncle Doc repeated the story of the snake and this time Charity was able to see that he wasn't laughing at her. She could even see the humor in the story herself. A thought ran through her mind that Will had only told the story to Uncle Doc because he wasn't upset by it. Then she saw again the expression on his face when the dismembered snake made him think of the war. And his declaration that he was determined to live here. Still, she thought she understood the feelings of the unknown Carl Dietz maybe better than she did the nonjudgmental emotions that the other three at the table seemed to have.

"Would you, Charity?" The question seemed to come out of thin air and Charity realized that she had been so deep in thought that she had missed the first question.

"I'm sorry, Bethany. I wasn't attending."

"It's all right. I just asked if you'd like to see the wedding dress Nell and I are working on."

"I'd love to, Bethany. Is it almost done?"

"I'm just promising myself that I'll have it finished in time for the wedding. But, if you're through eating, let's go in our room now. Coming, Nell?"

"Thanks, Bethany. I'll just clean the dishes, then maybe work on my herbs awhile before it gets too dark. You two go on."

"I usually work on this at the table in the big room, but I just want to show it to you now and maybe take a few stitches." Bethany's face was soft with happiness as she drew a mound of finely woven white material from a chest beside her bed. As she spread it out on the bed,

Charity could see that the skirt was finished and a modest bodice soon would be.

Bethany took up her needle and sat down on the bed, adding a few stitches to the nearly finished tucking of the bodice as though she couldn't keep her hands off it.

"Can I help?" Charity asked, sitting down beside her.

"Thank you, Charity, but I just want every stitch to be mine. I feel like it's something I can do for Joshua. . .for our marriage. We've waited so long and now the war is over and his work seems to be here in the valley and. . .oh, I'm just so happy!"

"Joshua told me he met you during the war, but he didn't say how."

Bethany smiled. "It all seems so long ago now. But you know about the bushwhackers, the outliers?"

Charity nodded.

"During the war, bushwhackers came into the valley and just stole things and set barns on fire and generally acted like. . .well, you know how they are. They're still around. A lot of people hated Joshua because he preached against the war. He wasn't for North or South. He was for peace. Both sides thought that was wrong. The bushwhackers beat him unconscious and dumped him in the valley. I found him and Nell and I took care of him. Joshua and I fell in love. Charity, can you imagine how great it is that the war is over? But I'm being foolish. You suffered so much more than I did, losing your home and family. Forgive me." She put the material down and threw her arms about Charity.

"Of course I forgive you, Bethany, but the war won't be over for me until I find out what happened to my brother."

"I pray that you will, Charity. And you know that we'll keep trying. Every time Joshua goes out of the valley, he'll talk to people. And, Charity, Dad wasn't teasing you about the snake. Well, I admit he was teasing you, but he's very proud of you for taking care of yourself. I'm sure Will is, too."

Charity decided not to answer that. "Bethany, do you know Dave Bradley? He's been in the school a couple of times."

Bethany smiled. "I know Dave as much as it's possible to know him. He's. . .nobody quite knows him. . .where he stands on anything. He has the biggest farm in the valley. He went off to fight, but he hasn't said which side he fought on. He wasn't wounded and he came back before the war actually ended."

"He's going to get some of the men to help whitewash the inside of the school."

Bethany looked surprised, then thoughtful. "He does do things like that for us sometimes." She slipped her arm around Charity's shoulder again. "Or is it you that is bringing out his thoughtfulness?"

"Charity," Uncle Doc called from the other room, "can you come out? There's someone here to see you."

Charity and Bethany looked at each other. "Dave?" Charity whispered.

"Maybe. Let me just smooth your hair down a little. We mustn't take time to change your dress or he'll think you want to impress him. There, you look just fine."

Charity tried not to let her expression show her surprise that it was Will who stood by the table, his hand inside his shirt, where a small lump seemed to be alive. Charity felt her heart thump as a surge of something between anger and fear rushed through her.

Aunt Nell, who had been busy removing the pot of soup left from their supper from the small stove, turned and seemed to become aware of the moving lump inside Will's shirt.

"Willie Bowers, you don't have another snake in there? You just take it outside. Don't you dare try to give it to Charity."

"Oh, no, ma'am," Will said. "I wouldn't do that to Charity or," a hint of the laughter Charity had seen earlier appeared in his eyes, "a snake. I just thought that you might want to have something. . .friendlier. . .to kill the mice in the school. Anyway, I found this little guy out in the barn and I thought you might like it."

A sudden look of pain came over his face. He seemed to be struggling with the lump, which, as nearly as Charity could tell from his wince every time he pulled at it, had somehow attached itself to his body. At last, he pulled out a scrawny curl of black and white fur and stretched out claws.

"Ah, uh, it's a cat," he said, unnecessarily.

"And scared to death, poor thing," Aunt Nell said.

"Maybe we ought to be feeling sorry for Will instead of the cat," Uncle Doc said, with a twinkle. "He's the one who seems to be in pain."

Will managed a grin before the kitten jerked itself into an arc of color and landed on the floor, leaving a few streaks of red on his hand. It stood still for a minute, then raced off to investigate something under Aunt Nell's herb table.

Charity had simply been standing and watching, but

now she reacted. "I-I do like cats. And, thank you, Will. But it does seem a little wild, doesn't it?"

"More than a little, I think." Aunt Nell caught the cat midair as he leapt toward her herb table. He responded by grabbing at a sprig of plantain and catching it in one claw. "Wilder than wild, I think," she murmured, detaching the plant from his claw.

"I'll take it into my room. . .oh, no, it might tear Bethany's dress."

"I've put it away." Bethany had come to the door to see what the commotion was about. "And I think I heard his name."

"You did, Bethany?" Will asked. "I didn't."

"Wilder, of course. Could he have a better one?" She indicated the cat, who was now up on two legs batting at Charity's skirts.

"I think it fits him perfectly," Charity said, reaching down to scoop him up. A few gentle rubs around his ears with her finger made him relax a little against her, though he still followed any movement with his eyes.

"He likes you," Will said.

Charity didn't meet his eyes. "I'll take him in the other room," she said.

As she went out, she heard Uncle Doc say, "I'm thinking that it isn't just Wilder who likes my niece."

She closed the door before she heard anyone answer. She didn't want to hear anything that Will might have to say.

Bethany came in shortly afterward and smiled at the furry comma, who had quieted down and arranged himself on Charity's bed, but didn't remark on either the cat or Will's thoughtfulness.

Charity didn't go to sleep for a long time. It wasn't the cat or even the fact that Will had told the snake story, and she suspected she would have trouble sleeping for a long time.

Bethany had said that Joshua would inquire every time he went out of the valley for Daniel. But what could she do to find out what had happened to him?

seven

Charity stood near the door of the schoolhouse, watching Wilder paw at a piece of slate she had found and put on the pine table that would be her desk. "Don't you dare knock it off and break it," she threatened him, hurrying up the center aisle to rescue it.

Picking him up, she held him for a moment under her chin before he flew into a spraddled leap to the floor. He lived at the school now and met Charity each morning with loud complaints about being shut up alone. Occasionally, he had small unwelcome gifts to lay at her feet, but she saw and heard no more live mice. She thought he would be a link she could use to get to know her students and get them to accept her when they came in next week.

She turned and looked at the interior of the building. The fall sun seemed to reflect off the newly whitewashed logs. Somehow, Dave had found enough quicklime to put two coats on the time-grayed logs, something the valley folks told her hadn't been seen in the valley since the war started. She moved to the schoolhouse door, thinking of her last conversation with him, here where she stood now.

"You've turned it into a place the children will love. It's so light."

He smiled at her. "I'm just glad I can do something for them. . .and you. We need you here in the valley just as much as we need Nell and Doc."

She smiled back. "Now if only I could find my brother, I think I could be happy here."

"Perhaps I can help you with that. Where was your brother the last time you heard?"

She sighed. "It's been nearly two years. We had the last letter from him before Mama died. He was somewhere in Virginia then."

He looked at her intently. "What was his name? Morgan, of course, but what was his first name?"

"Daniel. Dan Morgan."

He looked away for a moment, then turned a controlled gaze back to her. "Do you think he might have come back to your old home in Tennessee?"

"The neighbors know where I am. I left him a letter with them. There's no house there anymore." She tried to keep the nostalgia out of her voice, but saw quick sympathy in his face.

Strange, she thought now, she hadn't seen Dave Bradley since that day. Nor had anyone else in the valley so far as she knew. But that was all right. She was just grateful that he had done so much to help her get the schoolhouse ready for her students and that she could get on Bethany's horse and ride home. She was grateful to Bethany for letting her have Rainbow today.

Before she could pull the door closed, she saw Will riding down the lane surrounded by three other men on horseback. Charity attempted to ignore the prickles that skimmed across the back of her head. There was something alarming about the men and she wasn't sure why. Their clothes from this distance looked to be about the same worn homespun that she was used to seeing in the valley.

As they got closer, she could see that they all wore beards of varying lengths and grooming. Maybe her feeling of dread was because they were with Will, who was riding between two of them followed by the third, or that they sat their horses with the practiced look she had seen in groups of soldiers. Perhaps they were Union buddies that Will was bringing to meet her for some reason of his own. Well, he could just take them away again. She might be changing a little toward Will, but that didn't mean she wanted to meet his friends.

Her thoughts were interrupted as they drew their horses to a stop in front of her and the man behind Will got down and walked toward her, while Will and the other two kept their places before her. The one coming toward her was a giant of a man, fully a foot taller than Charity and almost twice as wide.

He took off a shabby black hat. "Ma'am, are you Miss Charity Charlotte Morgan?"

"Why. . .why, yes I am," she said, perplexed, then hopeful. Did this have anything to do with Dave's or Joshua's promise to search for her brother? But why would Will be with them instead of Dave? And why ask her name? Will certainly knew who she was.

"Ma'am, is that your horse there?" The giant pointed to Rainbow, grazing just outside the schoolyard.

"Rainbow isn't mine, but I rode her down. I have to take her back. Bethany needs her."

So they were thieves, bushwhackers who had continued to prey on the people of the area, even after their excuse of the war was gone. And Will had shown his true colors by joining them. She thought, too late, of the gun that

Will had reloaded and left inside the schoolroom. She wished she could train it right on him now. She might even remind him that she knew how to shoot it. But, looking at the men, she knew it was too late to make any attempt to get to the gun.

She determined to defend Rainbow, disgusted that Will was participating in filching his old friend's horse. "You can't take her," she announced. "And you!" she glared at Will. "I'm appalled at you, stealing from your friends."

The men laughed and one of them put a gloved hand behind Will's back. Will opened his mouth, then looked at the man and closed it again without defending himself.

"No, ma'am," the man in front of her said, "you don't understand. We're not stealing the horse. We're stealing you for a friend. And the first thing we're to tell you is that you mustn't be afraid. You're not going to be hurt at all. Not at all, ma'am. But we want you to get on the horse and come with us."

"Why in the world do you want that?" Charity asked, looking directly at Will. He frowned and moved his head briefly but said nothing as the man beside him laughed and patted him on the back again.

"That you'll find out later. Just for now, we're going to take you and Will here to a place we know. You won't be hurt, ma'am," he repeated. "Don't be afraid. But, please get on your horse, ma'am. I don't want to have to force you."

"Well, you will have to force me. I have no intention of helping you take Rainbow. And it's silly to tell me that someone wants you to kidnap me. I don't have any money to make that worthwhile. Just you go on your way now. Why don't you just go on out of the valley, Will, and don't come back to make your parents ashamed?"

Again, Will didn't respond. The man before her did. "Excuse me, ma'am." He put his hat back on his head, then his arms reached out and he picked her up as easily as a mother lifting a baby.

Surprised, Charity didn't respond for a minute, then she tried to struggle, angry with her constricting skirts and the steel of his arms holding hers down. He deposited her on Rainbow's saddle without even breathing heavily.

"Now, ma'am," he said, "you'll be riding in front of me and behind old Will here." He laughed. "I won't hurt you at all, ma'am. I've been told to take good care of you. But you need to know that I do have a gun here and these other men do, too, so you'll be protected. We'll be going up the mountain, but don't try to ride off into the trees, for I won't let you. You might get lost." For the first time something close to a threatening note sounded in his voice.

They went around the schoolhouse and the men moved to single file with Will riding ahead of her, one of them riding behind him. They rode up the mountainside on a trail so faint that Charity wasn't sure it was a trail at all. In one place they had to ride around a mass of rhododendron, the green of their almond-shaped leaves contrasting with the vivid colors of the trees and the slick mixture of old and new leaves on the ground.

Charity was reminded of Will's anger that she rode Rainbow too fast across wet leaves on the lane. How could he pretend to care for the horse when he was a part of this. . . whatever it was?

They rode mostly in silence, though once in a while the giant who rode behind Charity called out a right or left turn.

When the trail widened as they rode across a shoulder of the mountain, Charity attempted to turn Rainbow, determined to ride back and confront the man.

He held up a big hand. "Turn around, ma'am, please," he said softly.

"I just want to talk to you," she said desperately. "Tell me why you're doing this. What does Will want?"

He laughed. "I'm only doing what I promised a friend to do. I only know you won't be hurt. I've been chosen and you're as safe with me as you'd be in a rocking chair at home. Please, ma'am, turn around."

Realizing that she wasn't going to get any further answer, she turned Rainbow's head and got back in line, noticing that Will and the two men were plodding on still in single file. She wished she had a stick of wood to hit Will as she had hit that Yankee captain back in Tennessee. Once again the thought of holding his own gun on him raced through her mind. She still knew that she couldn't shoot it at a man, but she wouldn't mind one bit scaring any one of these characters, especially Will.

The repeated assurances that she was safe told her that this must be something not a part of the usual outlier practices. Certainly they must know that they couldn't get any money for her. Could Will be kidnapping her in some kind of romantic plot? Did he think that spending some time alone up in the mountains would make him look better to her? Well, if he did, he was certainly wrong. She glared at his right shoulder, which was all she could see around the man and horse between them. He wouldn't dare turn and look her in the eye.

Then, as they moved higher up the mountain, she let

herself consider why she felt only anger instead of fear. That was Will riding up there before her. No matter what he had in mind, she knew instinctively that he wouldn't hurt her. Or was she trusting in God? She became aware that, underneath her thoughts, she had been praying, almost without realizing it, all the way up the mountain. Almost without words. Was this what Joshua spoke of as praying as easily as breathing? Was this the attitude that had made him capable of accepting whatever happened as he preached his beliefs?

Thinking about Joshua brought her to Aunt Nell and Uncle Doc. When would they miss her and what would they do? Would they think she'd suddenly decided to go back to Tennessee? If they did, she knew someone would look for her, but they'd never think that she'd gone up the mountain, never think that Will Bowers would do the terrible thing he was doing.

A halt in the horses in front of her brought her back to the present predicament. She could see nothing except another thicket of mountain laurel, but the men seemed to be discussing something. Shortly, they rode around the thicket and the man behind her spoke softly, telling her to follow them.

They seemed to be at the top of the mountain and a barely standing shanty looked like it grew up out of a wide shelf of rock and leaned against a cluster of trees. Someone could ride by the other side of the thicket and never know it was there.

They pulled their horses up in front of it.

"You'll get down now, ma'am, without my help."

Silently, Charity complied.

"Now go on in the house, ma'am. Just push on the door."

Charity walked past the other three men without looking at them. She was afraid she would explode if she met Will's downcast eyes. He didn't even have the nerve to direct her himself, but left it to this man with the deceptively soft voice.

The ill-fitting door moved to her hand, dragging against the floor as she opened it just enough to slip inside. She pulled it shut behind her.

Without taking time to examine the rickety table and one chair or the fur piled up to make a bed in the corner, she went directly below the one window. It was just an open hole in the wall. Whoever had stayed here before must have been tough enough to live with rain and cold.

But she didn't care who had been here before. She wasn't going to stay here now. She studied the window. It was small and too high for her to reach, but if she stood on that chair. . .She was pretty sure she could find her way back down to the valley, and then she'd tell Aunt Nell how right she had been about that Yankee, Will.

She picked the chair up and carried it across to the window, careful to not let it drag against the floor. She didn't know how close the men were, but she was sure that eventually someone, probably Will, would come in to tell her why she was here. If she was going out that window, there was no time to think about it. It had to be now.

The chair wobbled dangerously when she stood on it. For a minute she expected it to collapse, and she quickly inspected the window. If she could push a rotting piece of wood out, it would be a tight fit, but she could wriggle through. She was sure of it.

The wood came away in her hand. She could hear the men outside arguing about something in loud voices. It was now or never. She grasped the bottom of the window and, with a shove against the chair that pushed it back, she propelled herself into the opening. She didn't stop to see if the men heard the chair hit the floor. If one of them came in now, she would be trapped but in a very awkward position, with only her upper body outside.

Now, she realized two things—that she was going to have to go out the window head down, and that the cabin was perched dangerously on the narrow mountain top. Below her, she could see through the spaces between trees that everything was slanted down.

For a minute she considered trying to push herself back into the cabin. Then she refused. She wasn't going to be here when Will came in to tell her why he was doing what he was doing. She would roll when she hit, the way she and her childhood friends had learned to roll when they jumped out of trees back home.

Without giving herself time to think anymore, she pushed hard with both elbows and was suddenly falling, sliding, tumbling over and over, feeling branches and briars tearing at her clothes and skin. She stopped with an agonizing jolt of her left ribs against a jagged rock. She lay still for a minute, trying to get breath into her lungs.

The sound of shots back at the cabin forced her up and running. Feeling like her ribs were being crushed into her lungs, she stumbled against a tree, then felt her way around it. She heard someone coming behind her and shoved herself away, weaving through the trees, the piles of leaves under her feet making her feel like she was racing on something less solid than the earth.

Whoever was chasing her was getting closer and she couldn't get up any more speed. Her legs were refusing to move even as fast as before. Someone was right behind her. She felt herself being shoved to the ground.

"Charity, stop. You're running the wrong way."

eight

It took Charity a minute to realize that her assailant was Will. Then she struggled even harder. She was never going to let him take her back to that cabin.

"Charity, please. They're chasing us. You'll never be able to outrun them. We have to hide."

For a minute she only heard random sounds coming in between his panting breaths. Then the sounds formed words in her mind, and she was so surprised that she stopped struggling. He took advantage of her stillness to push her under the lip of a jutting rock.

"They're chasing me? You're the only one I see chasing me. You're in with some awful bunch of outliers."

"Hush, Charity, please. And be still. If we're quiet, they may go on by. We'll talk later."

"We won't ever talk again, Will Bowers. When I get back to Aunt Nell's—"

A hand, no longer gentle, covered her mouth. In the silence, she heard the crash of big feet running a little to the left of them. By the noise he was making smashing through bushes and starting rocks to rolling, she figured it must be the big man who had ridden behind her.

She indicated by nodding her head that she heard the man and would be silent. Will's hand moved from her mouth to clasp her hand. In spite of her anger with him, she found the touch surprisingly comforting.

Now that she was quiet, she was aware of the pain shooting through her body. It almost, but not quite, overwhelmed her anger with Will. But she wasn't going to move away from him yet. The sounds beside them told her that common sense was to stay where she was.

The sound of the blundering giant's running died away down the mountainside and they heard someone, no less noisy, coming behind him.

"Two," Will whispered low in her ear. "Let's see if the other man is coming."

After hearing no one for several minutes, Will whispered again, "They've left one up there. That means we can't get to the horses. We'll have to walk home."

"We?" She snapped, forcing herself not to yell at him. "Will, you helped them kidnap me. Now you're going to take me home?"

"Charity, I can't explain now. We have to get away before they realize they've lost us and come back. Just trust me and come on."

Without waiting for an answer, he slid out of their shelter and pulled her with him. Charity felt the jutting rock rake her sore arms and realized that it was the same rock she had crashed into when she fell down the mountain. If she had been lucky enough to fall into the space under it, even Will wouldn't have been able to find her. She must have been running in a circle. *God*, she thought, *why didn't You let me hide there*?

But the pain in her body took over and pushed out any thoughts. Everything hurt. She tried to take a step and stopped, choking with pain.

"Come on," Will's voice was hard, with no hint of any

compassion. "I know you hurt, but we have to get away."

Charity had nothing left inside to challenge him. She allowed him to pull her along for a few steps and then, determined to move on her own no matter what the pain, she attempted to pull her hand from his.

He held it tighter. "It's getting dark. We could get separated easily in these trees."

I want to get away from you, she thought. But she left her hand in his, noticing once more, that she felt a comfort there.

"Do we have to go up?" she whispered.

"Just for a little while," he said briefly, without slowing down. "Home is on the other side of the mountain. Hush, now." For a minute, something in his voice reminded her of some faraway childhood admonition from her brother. Then she heard a sharpness in his voice. "Quiet." The gentleness was gone. The word was a flat command.

She tried to drop her hand from his and felt his squeeze down in a grip that made her aware of every little cut. They were on top of the mountain now, and she could make out blurred forms of the horses and the cabin in the dimness. Accepting the need for silence, she stopped trying to get her hand away from his and concentrated on walking as noiselessly as possible, ignoring a spot on top of her left foot that must be leaving blood on her stocking.

After a bit, they moved out of sight of the horses and started going down. At first, it seemed easier to Charity, then, as they walked down an especially steep slope, she realized that pushing against the tilt of the ground made her legs hurt more than ever.

She pulled against Will's hand. "I've got to stop."

He turned back to her, seeming now to realize how exhausted she was. "All right. I think we're far enough away that they won't find us now. Especially since it's getting dark and they're probably still looking on the other side of the mountain. It's really lucky that you led them the wrong way."

He led her to a big rock and sat down beside her. "I'm sorry I don't have anything to cushion the rock," he said. "Or to keep you warmer. It's going to get colder on the way home. For now, while you're resting, we need to talk."

She was too tired and hurting too badly to hold on to her anger. "All right. Just tell me why you did this. And who were those men?"

She heard a sharp intake of breath before he answered. "Charity Charlotte Morgan, I know you've been mad at me more than not, but how can you think I'd get involved in a stupid thing like carrying you off up this mountain? Not to mention a dangerous thing. I wasn't with those men. I was being threatened just like you were. That man beside me had a knife against my back. Just to remind me, he said, that if I made any trouble, it would be you he'd use it on."

She sat silently for several minutes, and he let her have time to consider. "Why did they want you? And why me?"

"Does that question mean you believe me?"

"I just want to hear your answer."

He sighed again. "It wasn't me they wanted. It was you. I just happened to be coming into the valley when they did, planning to stop by the school to see if you were still there, and they took me along to keep me quiet. They told me that if I made any attempt to help you or get away, you would be hurt. I couldn't do anything till the big guy went into the cabin and found you gone. Then I ran. If you heard the shots, it was me they were shooting at. I followed you by the broken branches and shrubs you must have rolled over." His voice took on sympathy. "I know you must be hurting."

She considered that for a minute. "Almost everywhere." Then she added, "All right, I believe you. After all, you helped me get away. Or are helping me. But who are they and why did they want me? Is it the school?"

"From what I heard, it has something to do with Dave Bradley. Oh, not that he wants to hurt you," he said quickly as she sat up straighter, then moaned as her muscles jerked. "They seemed to think that taking you up there would make him do something for them or at least be pleased with them. I'm not sure, but," a note of something—was it jealousy—crept into his voice, "anyway, they seemed to think that he's. . .sweet on you."

She decided not to answer. Sweet on her? Dave had done several things for her, but was it for her or for the school? He hadn't made any attempt to call on her or even be alone with her, and she didn't think she wanted him to.

"Are we lost? I can't even see you anymore. Do we have to stay on this mountain till morning?"

He seemed as relieved as she to change the subject. He even laughed. "I've hunted this mountain since I was little. You couldn't lose me in a blizzard. We can easy get home before morning if you feel like walking. If you don't, I know a cave where you can sleep, but it will be chilly. And we'll have to eat whatever I can find on the land for breakfast."

She shuddered. "Let's walk. I just want to get to my own bed and have Aunt Nell massage some of her herbs into my bruises. Besides, she must be frantic by now."

"All right. Do you think you can walk now?"

In answer she stood up, holding herself away from him so he couldn't feel her sway. "I'm ready."

"I'm going to keep you beside me as much as possible. If we have to go single file, hold on to my shirt. There's no moon and it's going to be black as a sack of black cats."

"Will, I discovered riding up the mountain with those men that I was praying without even being totally aware of it. I think I want to pray now on purpose."

He stopped and caught her hand. "I was, too, Charity. I think I made a lot of promises if you wouldn't be hurt."

They held hands and prayed silently. Charity found herself not only feeling close to God but accepting a closeness to Will that she had never felt with anyone before. His gentle pressure on her hands told her that he shared the bond. After a short while, he let her left hand go and, holding her other hand close, started down. Totally trusting him, she followed.

It was a nightmare trip down the mountain. At times Charity thought getting down wasn't worth it. She just wanted to lie down on whatever stack of leaves was handy and stay there forever. Her whole being was contained in her legs, every step a result of a definite command from her brain. She had never been so aware of the mechanics of walking. Talking was so far from necessary or even possible that she didn't even attempt it.

But Will did. Even when her tired brain couldn't recognize words, she heard his voice, his tones, felt his hand sheltering hers. Finally, no matter what he might be saying, she heard only words entwining with her thoughts, *you can, you can, you can.*

It was hours later, as they came out into a small clearing, that a glimpse of light below them looked like something as big as the sun to her.

"Look, Will," she gasped. "Look."

"I know. That's my house. That's Mama's candle that we're seeing there through the trees. Don't you recognize this place? Well, I guess you wouldn't in the dark. This is where I found out for the first time how stubborn you are. You've done it, Charity. A little bit more and you'll be able to see Doc's house. And I'll bet you'll see a light there, too."

The light gave Charity a boost and she felt herself pushing Will to walk faster as they went through the clearing and into the trees again.

"Will?"

"Charity."

"I'm sorry that I thought you'd be one of that bunch."

She heard a chuckle as he squeezed her hand. "This whole thing was almost worth it just to hear you say you're sorry. You didn't even say that about Dad's poor little snake."

"Big snake."

He sobered. "I don't blame you, Charity. You couldn't tell that I wasn't one of them. But Dave Bradley has got some explaining to do when he comes back. If he does."

She didn't answer, putting all her energy into the last bit of walking. Now the refrain in her mind changed to *get to Birdsong Road, get to Birdsong Road. Almost there. Almost there.*

She felt as if she could almost run as she followed Will. They were so close. Her feet seemed to be rising high off the ground with each step, though the drag of the grass under them told her that she was barely moving them. Wanting to show herself that she could, she forced one foot high and came down in a depression and felt herself twisting, falling against Will.

He turned and caught her in his arms before she could hit the ground, holding her tightly until she got her fight against gravity in control.

As she pulled herself to a full standing position, he didn't turn her loose. Out of the darkness, she felt his face lowering toward hers and instinctively looked up. His mouth touched hers gently, then was gone almost before she could breathe.

"Are you all right?" His voice sounded as ordinary as though he hadn't just kissed her. "Did you hurt your ankle? Can you walk all right? I can carry you down."

She tried to reply in the same tone of voice. Had he really kissed her? It was almost as if a moth had flown through the night and touched her lips. And was her breathing so short because of the kiss or the torture of their trip down? She decided she was too exhausted to try to sort it out now. She was having to hold back tears of fatigue, of pain, and the gentle caring that kiss had shown made it even more difficult.

She put her foot to the ground and felt a sharper pain. "But it's not that bad," she assured both him and herself between tight lips. "I can walk."

"It's not far now. If it weren't so dark, you could see Birdsong Road. We'll take it slow and easy." He kept one arm around her as they started walking again. "And it's wide enough here that I can help you."

She didn't reply. Being able to lean on him after the torturous trip down was like finding someone to lean on after the horrible things that had happened back in Tennessee. For just this short way to home, she could give up her need for independence.

"Child." Aunt Nell met them, carrying a lantern. She caught Charity in her arms. "Where have you been? We've been worried sick, trying to find you. Doc and Joshua and Bethany are out now, going all over the valley."

Her look at Will was close to a glare.

"Oh, Aunt Nell. . .Aunt Nell! I left Wilder down there in the school. And I don't think I thought to close the door. He'll wander off and get lost. . .or killed."

"Sweetheart, we can't worry about a cat now." Aunt Nell let her strong fingers drift over Charity's face, pressing gently on each puffy bruise and scratch. "Come inside, now, and let me take care of those bruises. And you're limping. Will, you come in, too. You can tell me what happened while I warm up some balsam." All the time she was talking, Aunt Nell was guiding Charity inside and to the bed at the end of the room.

Too tired and full of pain to argue, Charity let Will explain what had happened while Aunt Nell gently washed her face and arms with some soothing mixture. Then Aunt Nell shooed Will home before she went to work on the leg. Will left, Charity realized, without mentioning that he thought the kidnapping had something to do with Dave Bradley. She wondered why, but her mind was too tired to think anymore about it or about Wilder.

Sometime later she heard Aunt Nell and the others talking, but she couldn't wake up enough to concentrate on their words.

She was awakened by Aunt Nell's gentle touch on her forehead. "Charity, I know you're not going to want to move any part of your body this morning, but Dave Bradley is here. I told him you were recovering from last night's ordeal and," she stopped talking and stood thinking for a minute, "you know, he seemed to already know about it. Was he with you?"

She sat on the bed, gently massaging Charity's arm muscles. "Never mind. I know you're still fuzzy about it all. We'll just see if you can stand on that ankle in a little bit. Dave's waiting on the porch till we get you presentable. Hmm, that ankle's a little swollen."

All the time she was talking, she was working an ointment into Charity's bruises, coming at last to the ankle. Charity simply told herself to relax until Aunt Nell was through and appreciated that she wasn't being pushed to talk. She only moved when Aunt Nell indicated she needed to. She noticed then that, though the first movement of a muscle was torture, much of the pain was gone after the herbal massage. When Aunt Nell placed her arm behind her shoulders and assisted her to sit up, she felt fairly comfortable and turned herself to bring her feet to the floor.

"All right," Aunt Nell said, almost to herself, "now we'll see." She helped Charity rise to her feet.

There was a moment of pain. She groaned and eased herself back to a sitting position.

"It really isn't that bad," she assured Aunt Nell. "It was just that first pressure."

"You're sure? Because we'll keep you off your feet if it hurts. Move it back and forth while you're sitting down and then we'll try one more time. If it still hurts, we'll just keep you here. Dave can come back later."

"No. I want to talk to him today. It isn't that bad."

Aunt Nell looked at her sharply, but didn't comment. She gently guided the ankle into a series of circles, watching Charity's face carefully.

Charity stood again, forcing herself not to grimace with the pain. "It's better. I can do it."

"We'll try walking into your room so you can get dressed. Then we'll decide about seeing Dave."

Charity took a step, keeping her expression carefully controlled as she felt a milder pain in her ankle. She had to see Dave. He had to tell her why that wild experience had happened yesterday.

She managed to walk with only a bare limp and, though Charity knew she wasn't really fooling her, Aunt Nell led her into her room and brought her clothes to her from her chest. Charity quickly dressed and went back into the other room, where Aunt Nell seated her by the empty fireplace, with her foot on a low stool, and went to get Dave.

Dave's handsome face was concerned as he came toward her. "I'm so sorry, Charity. I wouldn't have had you hurt yesterday for anything."

"Perhaps you can tell us why yesterday happened." Aunt Nell motioned him to a chair, but without the welcoming smile with which she usually greeted people. "Charity was too tired and sore to talk much last night or this morning, but you must have had something to do with it or you wouldn't be here now."

"I didn't plan it, but, yes, I do know about it." He looked from Aunt Nell to Charity. He stood up abruptly and walked over to look out the door. Then he turned back. "Charity, I'm sorry. I tried to get to the school and explain everything to you, but I was too late. The men who took you up there didn't know themselves why they were doing it. All they knew was that you were not to be hurt or frightened. They were just following orders, and they aren't the smartest people who ever rode a horse. And they were thrown off course when they discovered that Will was going to the school. It was meant to be a happy time for you, Charity."

"Happy?" The word was close to a snort in Aunt Nell's mouth.

"Yes." He turned and faced them, something close to a smile playing about his mouth. "To see your brother."

nine

"Daniel?" Charity could hardly speak. "Daniel. . .Daniel is alive? You know where he is? Oh, oh, thank you, God. Dave, thank you."

She stood, not recognizing the pain of her ankle as she rushed over to give Dave the hug she wanted to give Daniel.

Dave smiled down at her, then gently removed her arms and helped her back to her chair. Then he knelt beside her and took her hand, while Aunt Nell looked at him with a mixture of happiness and challenge in her expression.

"Explain yourself, Dave," she said firmly. "If Daniel is alive and you know where he is, why have you let Charity grieve all these weeks?"

"I'll tell you as much as I can," Dave said soberly. "Daniel was a Confederate spy during the war. There was a time when his activities caused. . .well, Miss Charity, you need not hear the details, but enough trouble that he is now considered to be an enemy of the United States even though the war is over. He has to hide. The easiest place to hide now is with the groups of men still roaming the hills. I know something of your brother's caliber, Miss Charity, and I know that he can never be one of them. Nell, I know you don't have good feelings about these men since they're some of the same men who used to come raiding the valley."

"Dave, you helped us fight back against these men. Why are you with them now?"

"I'm not with them, Nell. I was aware of Daniel Morgan through. . .my own activities in the war."

"You were a spy?"

Dave was quiet for a moment. "Not for the Confederacy, Nell."

"For the Union?"

He nodded.

"You. . .you're a Yankee, too." Charity drew as far away from him as possible without standing on her now throbbing ankle.

"Not now, Charity. I live here in this valley."

"You and my brother were on opposite sides. You would have killed him if you had found him."

Dave didn't answer for a moment. Then, quietly, "If I had found him then, yes. I hunted him. He was causing Union men to die. But, Charity, the war is over. I don't know exactly where he is now, but I have contacts, still. That's how I got word to him that you are here. The plan was for him to be there when you arrived, but he had to dodge a bounty hunter and it delayed him. Then you were so independent and brave, Charity."

Tears filled Charity's eyes. "To think that I could have seen Daniel if I'd only stayed there. But he's alive, Aunt Nell. He's alive. Oh, Aunt Nell, I'm so happy."

"But what do we do now? He can't stay with those. . . men."

"I'll keep trying to find him," Dave said. "Charity, don't look like that. I've thought about it and I want to try to get him safely here. Here is the only place I can think of where he can be safe and be with you. He can't ever go back to your home in Tennessee. They're watching it. We could hide him. Give him a new name."

"Give who a new name?" Uncle Doc stood in the open door, his medical bag in his hand. "And why has Charity been crying?"

"Oh, Uncle Doc, it's happy crying. Daniel is alive. I want to run and shout even if my ankle hurts."

"Wait, Charity. Let's not shout, yet. In fact, I think that we need to keep it quiet that Daniel's alive. No more than us, Bethany, and Joshua. . ." Aunt Nell stood in thought for a moment. "And Will to keep him from confronting Dave about the kidnapping."

Charity gasped, suddenly hearing again Will's tirade against the Confederate spy named Morgan. Daniel. Daniel was the spy he was talking about who gave the information that caused Will's company to be nearly wiped out.

She felt a moment of fierce pride. Daniel had been a factor in punishing the Yankees who drove themselves into the body of the South like a sword. Then it changed to sorrow as she felt tears in her eyes again. Daniel Morgan had been a peaceful man, a song leader for their church, a loving brother, and the only father she'd ever known. Will had said he was the instrument of so many deaths. Remembering the sickness on Will's face, she felt an unspoken cry forming somewhere in some space deep inside her. *Someone I love caused Will to lose his companions.*

"Will mustn't know, Aunt Nell. Don't let Will know. He wants to punish Daniel." As briefly as possible, she told them what Will had said that day down at the school.

"I can't believe that the boy I've always known could talk to you like that."

"The war changed us all, Nell. In some way." Uncle Doc jumped into the conversation, still holding his medical bag.

"Aunt Nell, he was just so. . .it just seemed to spill out. . . he said he was sorry. And, anyway, he's a Yankee."

Dave nodded. "So was I, Charity. But I agree that if we're going to get Daniel back here, we mustn't let it be generally known who he is. Not even that he's your brother, Charity. And definitely Will can't know. I'll talk to him about what happened. Let him think the men weren't acting on my say-so. Which is true."

"Now, will someone please tell me what you are all talking about?" Uncle Doc set his bag down on the table and moved over to give Aunt Nell a quick kiss. "Whatever else, I'm glad to hear that your nephew is alive," he said.

Quickly, Aunt Nell explained the situation to him, as Dave, with a pat on Charity's arm, stood up to face him.

"So, you were a Northern spy. Some valley people suspected that there was something more than just being a regular soldier in your story. Or rather your silence. Now how do you plan to prove to us that you aren't still hunting Daniel Morgan to turn him over to those vultures that are coming down from the North to take advantage of the Southern defeat?"

Charity took in a choked-off breath. She hadn't thought to question Dave's motives. And he had admitted that he had spied for the North. What if he was lying?

"I'm not asking you for anything, Dr. Andrews. There's no information you can give me. All you can do is hide him if I find him and bring him here."

"Well, of course we'll do that," Uncle Doc said firmly.

Dave left soon after telling them that he had brought Rainbow and Will's horse back. "I turned Bowers's horse loose and let him find his way home. Rainbow is in the stable."

Aunt Nell insisted that Charity sit still with her ankle on a footstool while she prepared their lunch. Charity sat in a delicious glow, hardly noticing what was going on in the room. Her thoughts were all on the fact that Daniel was alive and Dave would find him for her. Then, to her surprise, the face of Will Bowers suddenly slid between her images of Daniel and Dave. Will was so caring as they walked down the mountain. How could he be the one person she knew who wanted to destroy her brother?

Sometime after they ate, Will came by to see how she was feeling. Charity tried hard to respond as naturally as possible to his concerned questions and not let her expression show what she was celebrating in her mind. He must never know what she now knew.

"I'm sorry I couldn't do anything to stop those men before they kidnapped you, Charity. But I promise you one thing. I'm going to find out why they did it. I promise you."

Please God, don't let him find out, Charity prayed in panic. Then she did what she could to stop him.

"Don't, Will. Whatever it was, it's over now. Maybe they just had the wrong person. Or, maybe it was just a prank on their part. A fun thing to scare the new schoolmarm. Anyway, I'm sure they'll never come around again."

It wasn't much, but it was all she could do without actually lying to him, and it didn't alter Will's determination.

"I'll find out. And I'll be with you if you go down to that school again before the children are there."

"Oh, I don't need to go down again, except to see about Wilder."

"I'll do that for you. In fact I'll stay there awhile with him. If they want to come back to see if you're there, I'll let them see my gun."

"Please take the gun with you when you leave, Will. The children will be there next week and I don't want them finding it."

He agreed and left soon after. The three of them were silent for a while, thinking their own thoughts.

Then Aunt Nell said sadly, "He's not the only one. There's others who'll feel the same way. Clyde McMillan has never got over losing his son even if Bertie McMillan has accepted being a widow and is doing a good job of raising little Sally without a father. Harry Lawrence. He lost an arm. Daniel may not be any safer here than anywhere else."

"Joshua can do it. It doesn't matter if they're Confederates or Yankees, everybody trusts him just like everybody trusts you two," Charity said. "But since he can't be my brother. . ." She let her voice trail off sadly.

"It's true. No one would question a friend that came to live with Joshua. . .except Will."

Charity blinked back unexpected tears. It didn't matter that Will had helped her escape from the men who kidnapped her. That glorious bond they had felt during the shared prayer could never happen again. The sweet kiss would be the only one. Even if he didn't know it, he was an enemy of her brother. And she had a secret she could never share with him.

ten

"I'm not averse to keeping information from some of our people in order to keep a man who fought for what he believed was right from prison or death," Joshua said. "And I'm sure, Nell, that anyone in your family is a worthwhile person. But we have to make our plans to be ready if Dave does find your brother." He turned to Charity. "What did he do before the war? What can we give out to the people as his reason for being here?"

"He was a farmer, of course, but he was a musician, too. He was the song leader in our church, and he played several instruments," Charity answered. She smiled to herself, remembering her happiness as, dressed in her prettiest Sunday clothes, she sat with her mother in their pew, watching her older brother line out the notes for the congregation.

Joshua's eyes brightened. "Can he teach shaped notes?" he asked eagerly.

"Oh, yes, that's what he did."

"Then we won't need to make up a reason for him to be here. He'll be our singing master. He'll bring a brightness, a joy to the community. The people love to sing, but not many of them can read notes. It may even bring in some of those neighbors who haven't forgiven each other enough to worship God together." Joshua's face saddened.

They were sitting in the big room of Uncle Doc and Aunt

Nell's cabin. Uncle Doc had built a fire much too large for the gentle evening and they had, two by two, moved their chairs away from the fireplace. As she watched Bethany and Joshua and then Aunt Nell and Uncle Doc move in unison, keeping their chairs close, Charity accepted a brief feeling of melancholy. How good it must be to be with someone dear.

She remembered that time of closeness on the mountain when she and Will seemed to be one, seeking God's support. And the brief softness of his kiss seemed to light on her lips again. But it was no good thinking of that now. He had declared himself forever an enemy.

Yet when she had declared enmity to him, as a Yankee, he had made efforts to win her over and she had almost forgotten her hostility that night on the mountain. Now it was all lost. Sadly, she wished that she and Will could take the path that her family and Dave seemed to be taking. The fighting was over, but the war lingered on as long as people hugged it to themselves.

❧

The Sunday service was scantily attended, and though the men and women sat on separate sides of the church as they had always done, now there was another, different separation, between North and South sympathizers.

Charity almost giggled when Uncle Doc ignored the men's side and, without any self-consciousness, walked in with Aunt Nell and sat beside her on the women's side. He drew Charity down beside him and Bethany sat on the other side of Aunt Nell.

Will came through the men's door with his father as Annie Bowers found a place behind Charity. She whispered to Charity, asking about her injuries from the trip down the mountain. As Charity turned to assure her that her ankle was only barely sore and the bruises were fading, she saw Will look almost with envy at Uncle Doc. He took a step toward her, then, unable to break the habit of his lifetime, sat beside his father on the men's side.

She noticed a distinct difference between the two sides, though she still wasn't sure about putting names to faces. The men seemed to listen to Joshua's sermon about a loving and forgiving God with angry faces, while those women whom she could see without turning around seemed to reflect the sentiment of his words. She didn't see Dave.

Before the benediction, Joshua announced that he had hopes of bringing in a songmaster for the church. As Charity heard the murmurs of approval from the congregation, she let herself give into the great joy of knowing that her brother was alive and she would be seeing him soon. For a moment she forgot the tight line they would all be walking to keep him safe.

Outside the church, in the soft richness of the autumn noontime, Will came over to her. "When your ankle is all well, I want to take you back up the mountain so you can see it without being scared," he said. "Maybe before you open the school."

Charity shook her head, glad to have an excuse not to spend a long time with him because of the secret she had to keep from him. "I'll be opening the school in two days," she said.

He touched her hand briefly. "Later then. On one of the days when there's no school."

Charity nodded, too busy trying to keep her response to

his touch from showing in her face to think of an answer.

❧

Nothing had been heard from Dave or Daniel by the following Tuesday when school was set to open. Charity was at school early, her hair carefully done up in a smooth knot to make her look as old as possible.

She took a minute to enjoy the fresh smell and brightness of the newly whitewashed logs before she set out the two new slates that Dave had found for her in Asheville and four old ones she had found in the schoolroom. She had broken the few pieces of chalk she had into shorter bits so that each of the five students she expected could have one. She put one of the new slates on her desk.

She was ready when her students arrived. As they crowded in together, she realized that they had assembled somewhere to prop up each other against the new experience. So much for getting to know each one as they came in.

She forced herself to not show any nervousness as she greeted them and allowed them to sit on whichever bench they chose. Maybe later, after she had learned the name of each child, she might seat them alphabetically or by their level of reading. They scattered themselves among the benches, none sitting close enough to suggest family or even friendship.

She had set the youngest age limit at four, thinking that some of the girls who cared for younger children at home might be able to come by, bringing them along. None of these looked that young, though. Charity guessed the oldest girl to be about ten, the youngest probably six.

She had just introduced herself and started to get names

of the children when a young woman appeared at the door holding a child of about three by the hand. She stopped at the door and waited for Charity to approach her.

"Did you want to enroll your little girl?" Charity smiled at the child, who had moved away from her mother's hand and was surveying the room and the other children with eyes that sparkled with intelligence. "She looks a little young."

"She's only three, but she asks questions that I can't answer." A shy smile flitted across the woman's face. "I thought. . .I thought that if I came and stayed with her. . .I'd learn to read with her and maybe. . .her dad could read but he was killed before she was born. . .in the war. I need to learn." She looked Charity directly eye to eye. "I want to learn for her."

Charity was immediately drawn to the woman, who didn't look old enough to have this child and to be a war widow. A picture of Will's face when she last saw him flitted through her mind. She wondered, *How can we ever learn to live with what the war has done to us?*

She heard herself mentally repeating the question as a prayer. *God, how can we ever learn to live with what the war has done to us*? And she felt a fragile belief that the question, addressed to God, could have an answer. She began to understand a little of the hope that kept Pastor Joshua Holt working in the community.

She turned her attention back to the woman. She hadn't thought of teaching students either this old or this young, but how could she refuse such a request?

"My name is Charity Morgan," she said, smiling at the two.

"I know," the woman said. "Mine is Bertie McMillan. Her name is Sally." She seemed to be waiting quietly for Charity's decision.

Charity heard herself speaking briskly, as if she were not still mentally groping for an answer. "We won't expect Sally to keep up with the rest of the children, but she must sit quietly so that she isn't a disturbance to them or to you. We will have you sit here on the last bench so that you can slip out if she gets restless."

"Thank you, ma'am." Bertie McMillan accepted Charity's implied requirement for her to be under Charity's control with a timid dignity that impressed Charity, even as she struggled with herself to allow this woman who may have been a year or two older to call her "ma'am." If she was going to require the other students to use the title, Bertie McMillan must use it also.

She turned to the other children, who had been watching them with expressions that ranged from wide-eyed interest to muffled giggles.

"Now, children," she said, mentally trying to set her face into the stern expression of Miss Jane, back in Nashville. Just then, Wilder came in from one of his hunting forays, jumped up onto the desk, and sat looking at them all very soberly. The children giggled, then joined Charity when she laughed out loud.

Was he telling her not to try to be Miss Jane but to be herself? She remembered how Miss Jane's pupils had longed for some sign that she saw them as people and responded to them individually. She didn't want these children to feel that way.

"Now, children," she repeated, "this is Wilder and he

lives here in the schoolroom, so we'll be seeing him a lot. But you can see by his expression that he wants all of us to learn. We will just learn each other's names today and you will show me how well you can read. Tomorrow we will start our real lessons."

She had each of them spell out their names on their slates as well as they could and found that three of the five could write their name. She gave the slate she had planned to use herself to be shared by Bertie and Sally. When she picked them up, there was a definite, if backward, SAL on the slate. Sally had somehow learned the first letters of her name. Perhaps she was as advanced as her mother seemed to think she was. Bertie had made no effort to write her own name.

Charity took the two blank slates and asked for names. She printed "MOLLY" and "JAMES" and returned the slates to the proper children, asking them to copy them as best they could. Without erasing Sally's attempt, she turned their slate over and gave Bertie her name to copy.

After giving them time to try, she encouraged their efforts and dismissed them, reminding them that they would have school each week on Tuesday, Wednesday, and Thursday. The children rushed out, glad to be free so soon.

Bertie and Sally were just moving toward the door when Dave appeared. He looked surprised, but greeted them by name and talked quietly with them for a few minutes, then waved good-bye to them.

"You know, Bertie is turning into a fine woman. She's willing to do anything for that child, even go to school with children."

"She seems to be a good mother," Charity said, glad that Dave seemed to respect Bertie's desire for education. Then she turned to the subject that was first in her heart. "Have you found Daniel?"

He shook his head. "No, but I've sent out a message by someone I can trust. It won't be long now. But, Charity, I've talked to Will. He seems to be willing to accept that the kidnapping was a mistake, but we talked some about war experiences. He is a threat to your brother. Will wouldn't have to hurt him himself. There are bounty hunters who'd be paid well by the government. They would be in here like lightning if he went to them."

Charity's eyes filled with tears. "What can we do?"

"I think," Dave looked down at her, "that it's up to you to keep Will from thinking about the new songmaster." He pressed her shoulder for a moment, then walked toward his horse.

Charity watched him ride away. What was he asking? That she use Will's feelings toward her to protect her brother? It didn't seem right. Yet, to protect her brother, to let him live the life he used to in a home, not hiding with a wild bunch of men, to let her see him even if she couldn't let anyone know he was her brother, would she do that? She silently bowed her head for a moment, unable to think of words for a prayer.

eleven

"Charity," Joshua Holt's voice was alive with excitement. He had stopped by the school just as all the students left. It was the second week of school and shortly before his wedding to Bethany.

Charity and her students had become comfortable with each other. Bertie and Sally were among her best students, and Charity had learned to respect Bertie's determination to learn to read in spite of some of the laughter being hidden behind spread hands of her neighbors. She had just bidden the mother and child a warm good-bye when Joshua rode in and swung down off his horse.

"What is it, Joshua? Is it. . . ?"

"It is." Joshua caught her hands and whirled them both about, making dry leaves swirl about their feet. "He will sing at our wedding and be introduced in church the next Sunday."

"Joshua, when can I see him? Will he stay with us? When is he coming?"

Joshua didn't answer her questions in the same order that she asked them. "He'll be staying with me until Bethany and I marry. Then he'll move into that empty cabin farther down our lane. He'll be right up against that mountain over on the other side of the valley from the one you took that trip up to see him." He hesitated. "That way, he can disappear quickly if it should become necessary."

Charity ignored the significance of his words. "But, when can I see him, Joshua?"

Joshua looked solemn. "I think that it will be correct for me to bring the new songmaster to meet Doc and Nell. . . and Bethany since he's to be our singer. And you and he can spend some time together, but be careful, Charity. Be very careful."

"When, Joshua? When?"

"Will a week from this evening be convenient?" His eyes held a teasing glint.

"Oh, Joshua, how can I live for a week before then? Have you seen him? How does he look?"

"If I can live for a week before I get to take Bethany into my home, surely you can wait for him. And yes, Dave took me to see him briefly, and he looks thin but strong. Perhaps older than when you last saw him."

"Oh, he hasn't turned gray, has he? Is his hair still red?"

Joshua laughed. "He looks like a candle on fire. That's the only resemblance I can see to you. And he will be a candle to the valley. I'm sure of it, having talked with him. But, Charity, the war and the way he's lived since then has had its effect on him, as well as on the rest of us. And something happened to his left leg. It's shorter than his right and he has a grave limp."

Charity felt her eyes fill with tears. "Oh, he's been hurt. How did he—?"

Joshua interrupted her question with a hug. "I don't know. We haven't talked about it or about his emotional state, but I know we will be friends. I hope I can be his support."

Charity refused Joshua's offer to ride home with him on

his horse. She was sure that he understood her desire to be alone. She walked up Birdsong Road without seeing anything of the fall leaves or flowers. Daniel was alive. Daniel was coming to live in the valley. How could she have let so much time go by without thanking God for his life?

But she waited until she came to her favorite place in the road, where the boughs of sugar maples met across the road to form a long arch high above. There, sunlight filtering through the yellow leaves always seemed to enclose her in a globe of ethereal color so uplifting that she needed no words to express her gratitude to God.

She wasn't sure how long she stayed in the glow of His world. She remembered the first time she came into the valley. She thought of Joshua's words that the sugar maples beside the school welcomed her. Now she was at home in the valley and Daniel would soon be there. If only Will could share her joy; if only he could know what a good man Daniel really was. It was the war. . .the war. *God, please help us get over this war.*

Refusing to let any sad thoughts interfere with her happiness, she continued on toward home, but, anxious as she was to tell Aunt Nell that Daniel was coming, she was glad that no one was there when she arrived. She wanted more time alone to think about seeing Daniel.

The weather cooled off in the next week, and ten-year-old James missed school to help his father get the last of the corn into the crib. Molly stayed home one day to help make apple butter. Charity fought to keep her mind on the primer that Bertie and Sally and two of the other children were learning together, at about the same speed, in spite of Sally's age.

When Dave came to the school at closing time on Thursday, she felt a wild whirligig of emotions. Was he going to tell her that Daniel was in the valley? That he wasn't coming?

To her surprise, he only nodded to her, but was there a special look in his eyes when he looked at her? Was that almost a wink?

Then he turned his attention to Bertie and Sally. From the easy way he swung Sally up to his shoulder and her delighted reaction, Charity realized that he must have been spending some time with them. She remembered his comment about Bertie's care for Sally. She hoped for Sally's sake that he and her mother might be finding an interest in each other.

"But don't forget about Daniel," she murmured to their departing backs.

When she hurried home, she found that he hadn't. When she entered the big room, she found Aunt Nell and Bethany putting an early supper on the table for Uncle Doc and Joshua and two other men. She rushed into the room as the tall, red-haired man stood up, holding out his arms. Daniel was there.

For a moment, while Uncle Doc rushed to close the door against outside eyes, they simply held each other; then came words, at first from both of them at once.

"You've grown inches. . ."

"You're so thin. . ."

"Your head's on fire, little sister."

"Oh, Daniel, I'm too big for that now."

Then, knowing what she had to tell him, she drew back. "Do you know about Mama?"

He nodded. "One of the. . .other operatives told me sometime after. I'm sorry I couldn't come. They were watching and I had things I had to do that, because of my position in the army, had to come first. I'm sorry, Charity. I know you had a hard time."

She nodded, not letting her arms drop from around him. "What you were doing was so much more important, Daniel. I stayed with the Wrights until Joshua came for me."

"I wonder." Nell stood with a bowl of bean soup in her hands. "I never knew who left me a letter telling me that your mother had died and Charity was alone. Was it you, Daniel?"

Before he could do more than nod, Joshua interrupted to introduce Brother John Hodges, the minister friend who would marry him and Bethany. After Charity had managed to get her mind off Daniel long enough to speak a few words to the amiable man, Joshua returned to Daniel's need for secrecy.

"We have to stop calling him Daniel. Both his names need to be changed. Have you decided who you are?" He turned to Daniel.

Daniel nodded soberly. "To answer your question, Joshua," he said thoughtfully, "yes, I know who I am and whose I am. I've asked forgiveness of our Lord for the hurt I may have caused to any of my fellow men. And I have received it."

He moved back to the table, his arm still around Charity. He pulled an empty chair close to his and pulled her down beside him. Nell dipped bean soup into their bowls, but no one picked up a spoon or bowed their heads for the grace.

"I've chosen a new name," Daniel added slowly, "and it's symbolic of my need to leave that life behind. The things I had to do—well, I never had to run across a battlefield shooting at my brothers, but I will have to live the rest of my life knowing that things I did caused others to do it. I've a lot of memories I wish I didn't have, but I know God will sustain me."

Charity felt the shadow in his eyes fill her mind as she thought of Will and the reason for his bitterness. She hoped that Daniel would never have to hear Will tell of his own experience with the results of Daniel's work. For a moment her happiness at being with Daniel dimmed. She could never be as close to Will again as she was on that frightening trip down the mountain in the dark. Then she turned her attention back to Daniel.

He was looking very serious. "I'm taking the names of two of Christ's disciples who changed their names when they changed their lives. I'll be Peter Matthews. And I pray that mine will be so changed that I will never again in any way be responsible for harm to another person."

Charity looked down to hide the tears in her eyes, then she looked at Bethany and Nell and saw answering tears in theirs. Even Joshua's looked suspiciously damp as he led them in a prayer of gratitude for Peter Matthews's safe return to a peaceful world and supplication for help with the rest of his life and that their neighbors might learn once again to be real neighbors to each other.

"Now," Uncle Doc said firmly, "we start this new life of his. Can we agree that, at the end of this meal, Charity will move away from Peter Matthews's side and will treat him like a stranger from that time on? Can you do that, Charity?"

"Start now," Nell said, a warning in her voice. "Will Bowers is on the porch. Don't move, Charity. He'll suspect something." She stood and strode to the door, opening it before Will could knock. She led him in and, everyone speaking at once, they managed to introduce John Hodges and Peter Matthews, the new songmaster who was to sing at the wedding.

Will delivered the cake his mother had sent for the wedding supper and left quickly, barely speaking to Charity. He was too observant not to pick up on the intense atmosphere in the room and Charity's attempts to control whatever emotion she thought should be showing on her face. He bowed his head as he walked back toward the Bowerses' house. No wonder Charity didn't seem interested in Dave. He must have dreamed that she showed some response to him up on the mountain that night.

Whatever was being hidden in that room, it had to do with the new songmaster, and Charity was too honest to be able to hide her feelings. She had known Peter Matthews before. And she loved him. It showed.

Was it some distant cousin with the same flaming hair who had followed her from Tennessee in order to claim her for his own?

Instead of going home, Will turned his feet toward the clearing where he had first met Charity. He stayed there until well after the trees darkened around him.

twelve

Saturday was clear and warm for late October. Bethany stayed at home until it was time to dress for the wedding. It was to be a simple ceremony, but they had invited everyone who lived in the valley and they expected most of them to come. The people of the valley had long ago taken Doc and Bethany Andrews into their hearts, and Nell had been their herb woman from her early youth.

Charity spent Saturday gathering her wedding gift of fall wildflowers, mostly asters and goldenrod, mixed with greenery and the red of magnolia cones and sprays of colorful leaves. She waited until the last minute to place them throughout the church, knowing that they would go limp quickly. She placed a large jar of the marvelous sugar maple leaves that had given her two such spiritual moments, aware that they had to be combined with sunshine to splash their miraculous color through the air, but Bethany and Joshua would recognize the symbolism. She barely got home in time to change to her one slightly worn Sunday dress.

"Oh, you look lovely, Bethany," she cried as she came into the big room and saw Bethany dressed in her simple white cotton dress. Its only ornamentation was rows of tucking down each side of the bodice. The material for the dress had been sent down from Asheville by Joshua's sister as her wedding present to the couple, but she had few resources and Bethany had to make the skirt less full than she would have chosen. However, Bethany's slim body gave it a look of elegance.

Charity gave her a small bouquet of white ladies' tresses to carry, just as Dave drove up in his buggy, pulled by a rangy gray. His gift to the couple was to carry Bethany to the wedding.

Charity quickly changed and walked with Uncle Doc and Aunt Nell. Aunt Nell was wearing her own Sunday best, which looked very little different from the shapeless linsey-woolseys that she wore every day. Uncle Doc was dressed in a dark coat and pants that Charity was sure had gone out of style years ago. The suit was a bit tight about the waist, but he still managed to look elegant in it.

. As they walked to the church, they were joined, one or two at a time, by the valley families, wearing an assortment of garments from well-washed everyday working clothes to one or two dresses with wide skirts and a bit of lace on the bodice.

But everything showed the signs of age. The nicest of the dresses were faded or yellowed. For a moment, Charity remembered her life in Tennessee before the war, when Miss Simpson, the seamstress, was kept busy year-round with new dresses for the ladies and their daughters. She wished fervently that she could bring in new material, new people to sew, just to bring some joy to these people who were trying so hard to live with the pain that the outside world had brought to them by starting a war.

Once again Uncle Doc broke precedent by striding in and sitting with Aunt Nell and Charity on the women's side of the church. Dave did the same, sitting by Bertie and Sally, ignoring the looks of their neighbors.

Charity saw Will come in and sit with his father on the men's side and, for a moment, let herself wonder if he would sit on the women's side to be close to her. . .if they could ever be close.

Her attention was caught by a glimpse of a large woman in mismatched clothes who came in at the last minute. Several women moved to make room for her at the end of one of the benches and, as she sat down, Charity forced herself not to stare at her bare feet.

She allowed her gaze to rest on the back of Daniel's. . . Peter's. . .head as he sat on the front bench with John Hodges. She could look at him now because everyone in there was looking at them and whispering among themselves, asking which of the two strangers was the new songmaster.

The congregation settled down with an audible bustle as the Reverend John Hodges stood and walked to the front of the center aisle. They turned as one to watch Joshua and Bethany walk up the aisle together, their faces seeming to project and return to each other the glow of perfect happiness and confidence, even as they faced the minister and their future waiting at the end of the aisle.

After they repeated the simple vows, they sat with the minister on the front bench while Peter moved to the bare pulpit and sang "Oh, Be Joyful in the Lord," then lined it out for the delighted congregation to sing. He led them through the song, denoting the melody by moving his arm up and down, slowly or more rapidly, according to the time. They went through it once again.

The congregation responded enthusiastically and he

turned to familiar hymns that took them back to life before the war. Looking around her at the radiant faces, Charity realized that her brother had brought more joy to them with his nonmaterial gift than she could have by bringing in cloth for new and stylish clothes.

After the ceremony, Dave drove the couple back to Uncle Doc's house, where simple refreshments of herbal tea and cake were served to the few neighbors who followed them. Charity noticed with a deep sadness that many of the valley neighbors still refused to meet socially with each other. The spirited singing at the church wasn't enough to change that. She noticed, with a twinge that she tried hard to suppress, that although Annie and Samuel Bowers were there, Will wasn't.

Bethany changed to one of her everyday dresses and she and Joshua chose to walk down the valley to their new home, accompanied by a few of their neighbors, who left them at their door. Sally was delighted to leave with Dave and her mother to be driven home in his buggy.

Charity watched her brother get on his horse and leave with John Hodges. She wished desperately that she could kiss him good night.

"Aunt Nell," she said, after everyone was gone, "who was the big woman who came in almost at the last minute? I noticed her because she was barefooted and I've never seen anyone come into a church barefooted before. But she seemed to have more friends among the women than anyone. . .except you and Bethany."

Aunt Nell laughed. "That's Mattie. She's a friend of ours who lives alone up on the mountain because she wants to and wears what she chooses. She used to pretend to know things that normal people didn't—where to find lost things and such, just to get people to come up to see her—but she doesn't do that anymore. And now people go up just to talk to her. . .when she chooses to be found. Bethany and Joshua are especially fond of her. Bethany rides up to see her pretty often. . .and she always is there for Bethany."

Charity, her curiosity satisfied, offered to clean up, and Aunt Nell, wisely knowing that she needed the physical activity, thanked her and retired with Uncle Doc to their room. While she was heating water to wash dishes, Charity heard someone call to Aunt Nell to come for a birth.

She let her thoughts run on the idea of the continuation of life come war or pestilence and forced herself to think only of her gratitude that her brother was near and not to think of Will at all.

thirteen

"Will, a bounty hunter who's looking for Morgan came in here to see me. He'd heard I'm bent on finding him. He'll pay me if I turn anything up. The money looks good in the shape I'm in, but getting it from giving Morgan his due looks even better."

Will felt his legs slam back against the rungs of the straight chair he was sitting in. He was in a sparsely furnished Asheville boardinghouse room where Rance Hunt, a war comrade, lived.

He had left Falling Water Valley immediately after the wedding, refusing to watch Charity look at the redheaded stranger who was so obviously not a stranger to her, refusing to think about the possibility that the next wedding might be theirs.

He had camped twice on the way into Asheville, not in any hurry to get there, yet thinking that somewhere he might get some idea of why Charity had been kidnapped. Dave hadn't given him any information other than that they were outliers, and he already knew that. Dave's suggestion that mistakes had been made and his declaration that he had never sent the men didn't convince him.

Once in Asheville, he had asked around until he found Rance Hunt and called on him only to offer friendship to his wounded comrade.

"Is this bounty hunter anywhere near finding that man?"

Rance Hunt moved irritably in his chair. The chair, obviously once a rocker, had been fitted with iron wheels by someone so that it could be pushed, though with difficulty.

"He thinks that he's somewhere in this area, and they've heard that he's hiding with a bunch of outliers. He'll pay well for any kind of information on him. I'm looking, Will. I aim to make finding him my life—doing what I can do, which is to get all our old company looking for him. Mail is more dependable now that the war's over, and I'm sending letters out." He indicated a stack of torn pieces of paper on a table beside him. "I don't have much other life, not being able to walk on this one piece of a leg I have, but Mrs. Brown, she owns this house, mails out my letters for me."

"How can you tell anyone how to find him? You don't even know what he looks like."

"I do." Rance nodded. "The bounty hunter gave me a direct description of him. The main thing, the thing he can't hide, is his limp. Seems like some Union man found him and shot him, but he got away. We think the shot broke his leg and maybe it didn't heal right."

"Rance, half the men in the country have limps now."

"But half the men in the country aren't six feet four inches tall and redheaded. And the bounty man gave me his history, what he was before the war. Lived over in Tennessee. Williamson County. Just outside Nashville."

Will jerked himself out of his chair. He walked across the little room and pretended to stare out the window, but focused on dirt packed in one of the corners. Finally he was able to control his expression and turn back.

"He's from Williamson County?"

"Yeah, he was a well-to-do farmer there, big in the church, led the singing, prayed a lot. Wasn't married but had a mother and sister there. Big in the community."

Will didn't listen to any more. The awful truth was forcing itself into his mind. The new songmaster. Redheaded like Charity. Not Charity's sweetheart but her brother. Morgan. The man responsible for the deaths of his friends.

He hardly remembered leaving Rance Hunt. He knew that somehow he had managed not to promise to turn in Daniel Morgan if he ever found him. Not that he didn't want to see him pay for what he had done. But he needed time alone. The fact that Morgan was Charity's brother and Charity was keeping the secret from him only made the pain worse.

He camped once on the way back to Falling Water Valley, but he didn't go home. Instead, he turned his horse's head up the mountain, not sure when he would be ready to come down.

He rode aimlessly for two days, often repeating his paths of the day before, going across the mountain and for a way down the other side, eating little. Once he caught a small fish, cooked it on a stick, then left most of it for the crows. He chased a rabbit, then stopped and watched it run away, reluctant to kill the frightened animal. He chewed on sassafras twigs and drank water from Falling Water Creek. He slept on the ground and took nothing with him when he woke and moved on.

On the second evening he bedded down by the misty waterfall that gave the valley its name. He knew that there was a cave in the rock behind the waterfall, but he needed to be in the open. Just the thought of darkness coming on him in an enclosed place made him flinch. He turned his horse loose to graze and lay down close enough to the creek to hear it if he should wake in the night.

He woke angrily in the faint morning light from the pinch of a bare toe digging his shoulder. He rolled over and looked up into the bright blue eyes of the woman called Mattie, who'd lived up on this mountain since long before he could remember.

"I been watching you wander around for three days now. You lost?"

He sat up, not looking at her. "Yeah, I guess I am."

She laughed, a loud hoot. "Sure. You're little Willie Bowers, been all over this mountain all your living days."

"Will Bowers."

She hunkered down beside him, her shapeless dress dragging the ground around her bare feet. "So it's Will now. Willie not good enough, you need to change?"

"The war changed it."

"I remember the day you ran off to war. Thought it would be a big doins, didn't you?"

"I guess I did, Mattie. It wasn't."

"So what are you doing up here when everybody down in the valley is getting the last of the crops in?"

"My father did it without me while I was gone. He doesn't need me much now."

"Being needed. That's important. I pretended for a long time I could know things without being told so I'd be needed. I don't do that anymore since Joshua and Bethany helped me find God, and they understand that I live closer to Him by living here on the mountain. But I knew things then just from using my eyes and ears down in the valley and I still do. You're not running from not being needed. Not unless it's that schoolteacher not needing you, her having someone else come into the valley. I could tell you something about that, too, but I won't."

He picked up a stick and poked aimlessly at the creekside gravel. "What would you tell me if you had a mind to?"

She shook her head. "Charity's family to Joshua and Bethany."

"And you know something that might hurt her?" He put the stick down and looked at her.

She was silent, a stubborn look on her large face.

"You know who the songmaster is."

Not replying, she looked away into the trees.

"Mattie, I know who he is. He killed my friends." He felt the words in his throat like something he was unable to swallow, something that would lodge there for his lifetime.

She turned her gaze back to face him. "You won't hurt that family. Hurting that family won't bring your friends back. Won't get Charity off your mind, neither."

"I can get revenge for my friends. I can tell my friend in Asheville where he is. He'll get money from a bounty hunter. Money to buy him a real wheelchair, maybe a peg leg or crutches."

"Joshua said that down in Knoxville when he was there, they brought in a spy. They killed him and tried to hide his body from his family, but his family stole the body and buried it in their family cemetery. Think Charity can do that?"

"Those men I watched die didn't get buried in any family cemetery. They got rolled into one grave and what was left of us had to move on. They need to be avenged."

"Being somewhere where wars don't happen, your dead friends might could want some forgiving, instead of avenging. Think about it."

He turned his back on her, looking over the leaf color rampaging down the mountain.

When he turned back, she was gone, much too quietly for such a big woman.

He stood and moved over to his horse, surprised to see him nibbling at an ear of corn, while another lay in front of him. Leaving him there, Will walked over and watched the glint of sunrise color thread through the water, whistling its way down the mountain.

Revenge or forgiveness? Which would make the pain go away? He knew what the Bible would say. He'd heard about turning the other cheek from childhood, back before there was any need to think what it really meant, before his forbearance got torn away on the battlefields.

fourteen

"You know," Charity said to Aunt Nell, "I'm getting my kids interested in the stories in our books, but they don't care a bit about how words are spelled."

"Well, spelling words isn't much fun for them." Aunt Nell turned from her herb table, a sprig of parsley in her hand. "They could tell you a lot about how to hoe corn. But maybe we could make spelling fun for them. Why don't we have a spelling bee one of these evenings?"

"Oh, Aunt Nell, would you come?" Charity took her hands out of the pan of soapy water she was using to wash out a dress. "Would Uncle Doc?"

"Of course, and try to spell everyone down. Joshua and Bethany are going to Asheville to see his sister this week, but Bethany isn't much of a speller anyway. Want to do it Friday?"

"Friday? Can I get people to come that soon?"

"Honey, you could get people to come tomorrow if you could get the word around that quick. People here love to stand up and try to spell each other down. Almost as much as they love to sing. Why, we used to have. . ."

"What, Aunt Nell?" Charity put down the square of soap she had been rubbing against a berry stain on the skirt of her dress.

"That was before the war. Some of those people aren't even admitting that the rest of those people exist, or the rest of the people won't talk to the others of them."

"What, Aunt Nell?" Charity asked again.

Aunt Nell sighed. "Well, if that sentence was mixed up so is the neighborliness of this valley. Just get the word out, Charity, and we'll see who comes."

"I guess I can pull the side of the skirt over it," Charity said, looking unhappily at the stain, which wasn't even fading, "or hold my hand over it."

"What, Charity?" Aunt Nell asked over her shoulder.

"Never mind." Charity said, laughing. She was sure Aunt Nell would remind her to check for stains before putting the dress into the water, but it was too late now. She reached over to hug Aunt Nell with a wet hand. "I'm going to hang this out to get whatever sunshine is left, then I'll start supper."

"Fine. And Doc and I'll help you get people to the bee. I'll start with Lucy Ward. She'll spread it around."

Charity stretched her dress across a laurel bush, arranging it so the sun would hit the berry stain. Then she stood looking across to the trees that hid Will's house. She hadn't seen him since Bethany's wedding, and she had been afraid to talk to him then. What if something showed on her face when she looked at Daniel. . .Peter? *God*, she whispered, *help me to accept that I can't be close to Will for Daniel's. . . Peter's. . .sake.*

She went back inside and started putting together cornmeal and water for hoecakes. They would be good with the last of green beans from someone's garden, and she had an egg to beat into her batter.

Next year, she planned as she stirred the beans that she'd set to cook with onions earlier, *if I'm still here, I'll find a place by Aunt Nell's herbs to raise a garden of our own*. Aunt Nell was always too concerned with her herbs to think of raising anything else, and she and Uncle Doc and Bethany got enough from their patients to keep them in greens, but it would be nice to be able to choose what she cooked for once. Charity grinned proudly, thinking of how well she had learned to cook since coming to live with Aunt Nell. She had only watched their cook sometimes back in Tennessee.

☙

"So far, there's nobody here who's going to shoot anybody else," Aunt Nell whispered as Charity passed the bench where she sat with Uncle Doc and some of their neighbors.

"I hope not," Charity whispered back. "I'm nervous enough just thinking about trying to lead this spelling bee."

"Don't worry," Aunt Nell assured her. "You'll do fine. Everyone knows who'll win anyway."

Before Charity could ask her anything more, she turned her back to talk to Samuel Bowers. Charity reluctantly went up to her teacher's platform. Why had she agreed to this, anyway? Most of these people were older than she and undoubtedly laughing at the idea of someone her age trying to test them on their spelling ability.

She wished that Daniel. . .Peter. . .were here to support her, but she knew that he and Joshua had agreed that it wouldn't be wise for him to go anywhere but church until they were fairly sure that no Union sympathizer was going to recognize him. *No one like Will*, Charity thought, trying to control her expression against the pain that thought was causing.

As though thinking of him had brought him, Will came through the door. Without looking at her or greeting anyone, he sat on a back bench.

Charity stood speechless for an agonized moment. It was hard enough to stand up here and talk to the other faces, now quieted down and looking expectantly at her, much less know that Will was watching her. . .or was he? He seemed·to be looking around at the other people on the benches instead of her.

She drew in a shallow breath. Aunt Nell had carefully explained to her how it was to be done. She was nodding and smiling encouragingly now.

"If you are all ready," Charity began, noticing that Will was now looking at her, "I'm going to ask Aunt Nell and Dr. Andrews to choose up sides."

Aunt Nell and Uncle Doc moved to stand against opposite walls of the schoolhouse, their faces intense. Charity wrote a number on a slate and asked them both to guess.

"Eight," Uncle Doc said firmly.

Aunt Nell hesitated a moment, then guessed two.

Charity held up the slate with a big nine on it and the crowd, which seemed anxious for entertainment, laughed and clapped.

"Lucy Ward," he called.

Aunt Nell winced but called up Samuel Bowers, and they built up their teams with a satisfaction that showed how well they knew their neighbors. Charity noticed that Will, apparently not a great speller, was chosen among the last. Holding her spelling book in her hand, she announced the first word.

The first few, including Will, went down quickly, but

Charity found herself scrambling for harder words as three on each side joyfully sounded out words. Lucy Ward went down on "constable," and a woman she didn't know on Uncle Doc's side missed "seamstress." Now there were two on each side, and they were spelling words Charity admitted to herself that she couldn't have spelled if she didn't have them in front of her. "Apprentice," she called to Samuel Bowers, standing beside Aunt Nell.

"Ap. . .a, p. . .ren. . .a, p, r, e, n. . .t, i, c, e, apprentice," he spelled and pronounced the word by parts.

"No, I'm sorry, that's wrong." Charity checked the book again to be sure. The word went to Virgie Smith, on Uncle Doc's side. She changed the letters slightly but incorrectly, and Charity passed it to Aunt Nell, who spelled it easily.

It was down to Aunt Nell and Uncle Doc and, by the delighted expressions on everyone's face, Charity knew that this was what they had been waiting for.

Charity was turning the fragile pages of Uncle Doc's old wordbook now. He and Aunt Nell handled "wagonette" and "vestibule" with ease. Charity tried "gossamer" and "Monongahela" without getting either one out.

Flipping through alphabetically, Charity found "peripatetic" and called it out to Uncle Doc.

"Use it in a sentence," he challenged.

Charity glanced again at the book. "The peripatetic artist travels from town to town," she said.

"P, e, r, a. . .p, e, r." Uncle Doc stopped without finishing the spelling, his face showing that he recognized his mistake. With a triumphant expression that she didn't try to hide, Aunt Nell spelled it correctly.

Uncle Doc walked over and pretended to surrender.

Everyone clapped while they turned to cutting the cakes brought in by the women and helping Charity pass the slices out.

Will hardly paid attention to the spell down. He knew he could have spelled the word he went down on, but he wanted to be able to watch for Charity's brother. Where was he?

fifteen

"Did you notice that Johnny Myers and Vern Rogers edged closer together during the singing this morning than I've seen a Union and Confederate since the war started? They had to be remembering how they harmonized back then." Aunt Nell had settled herself beside Uncle Doc at the table, watching Charity doing her self-imposed task of setting out their Sunday supper. "That young nephew of mine is going to be a godsend to us. If anything will bring us back together, it will be singing, for we purely like to sing more than anything."

Uncle Doc looked thoughtful. "Nell, we did pretty good with the spell down. Why don't we try an all-day singing some Sunday?"

Aunt Nell nodded. "Good idea, and it will let Charity spend some time around her brother, too. Charity, I know how much it must hurt you not to be able to be close to him. You're handling it like a Morgan. I'm so proud of you."

Charity deftly flipped a hoecake in the big iron skillet, letting the procedure be an excuse not to look at her aunt. "I'm doing all right," she called over her shoulder.

Suddenly Aunt Nell was there, hugging her. "Charity, you're home. You don't have to pretend here."

Charity turned and snuggled inside Aunt Nell's arms, feeling the wetness of her own tears on Aunt Nell's dress. "Aunt Nell, I'm so afraid that I'll say something that lets people know who he is, I can't sleep at night. I don't know if I could keep it up all day."

Aunt Nell moved her away from the stove. "Child, don't worry that we'll do anything that makes it harder. The all-day singing was just an idea. If you don't want to, we won't."

Uncle Doc slipped past the two women and stoically began to remove the sizzling hoecakes from the skillet before they burned. Seeing him struggle with the wooden spatula, Aunt Nell and Charity untangled themselves. Aunt Nell took the spatula out of his hand and expertly slipped the bread onto a plate while Charity served up the vegetable stew.

After the grace, with complete understanding of each other's thinking, Uncle Doc and Aunt Nell started a conversation about some of the medical needs of the community, giving Charity time to be alone with her thoughts while being a part of their loving sphere.

❧

Monday was the kind of fall day that was so exquisite Charity felt a sense of frustration under her delight. Walking to school, she wanted to hold it in her hands, preserve it like the valley ladies canned their beans and berries, bury it in straw like potatoes, so she could pull it out and revel in it in January or just go in and look at it secure in its jar the way the ladies enjoyed walking by their shelves and admiring their summer's produce.

It wasn't a day to keep a group of mountain children inside a dusty schoolroom. She decided to have an outdoor lesson, one in which they might teach her as much as she taught them.

She was rewarded with smiles and giggles when she announced her plans to the children. Their excitement made her look forward to the day even more.

"Miss Charity, can we pick flowers?" Sally asked.

"Of course you may, Sally." Charity gently emphasized the word "may," but she was pretty sure Sally only heard that she was permitted to pick.

"Let's find some snakes," she heard James say, to her horror.

"Remember, children, that we must take care to keep our morning safe," she said, then aware of bland stares, thought how unnecessary the admonition was to a group of children raised here in these mountains. They had learned to live around snakes and wild animals.

As they filed out of the school into the soft stillness of the autumn day, she said, "Let's go see what we can find over by Falling Water Creek."

She wouldn't have far to herd the group of excited children, who were more interested in not being in the classroom than in the outdoors that they had lived with all their lives. But she had a different kind of teaching in mind.

When, with the help of Bertie, she had them settled on the bank of the creek, she explained that they were going to have a spelling class. She would send them off, one at a time, to find something to bring back to the class, telling them that the first one to correctly spell the name of the object got to go next.

Wisely, she sent Bertie and Sally first. Sally came back with a wild mustard plant, pulled up by the roots.

"Who can spell flower?" Charity asked.

"You mean flare, like Mama makes cakes with, Miss

Charity?" Molly asked.

"That's a good question, Molly," Charity said, ignoring her pronunciation. "The two words sound the same, but they mean something different. That is called a homonym. But we'll wait 'til later to talk about that. Right now, let's learn to spell what Sally is holding. Anyone want to try?"

"F-l-o-u-r," guessed Jane Warner.

"That's close, Jane, and that's what Molly's mama uses to bake her cake. This is different." She spelled out the word and went around the circle letting each child repeat the spelling.

Then, using the knowledge she had picked up from Aunt Nell, she took the plant apart and taught them to spell each of the parts.

"The petals are the prettiest," Sally said happily.

"They are, Sally, but the stems and roots are important to the flower just like corncakes are as important to us as the prettier cakes, but we like to have both, don't we?"

Since no one had spelled the word first, James held up his hand. "Can I go get the next thing, Miss Charity? I know where there's something good."

A little apprehensive, Charity agreed. What if he came back with something a ten-year-old would find interesting, like a snake? But she allowed him to go and he walked behind a cane break near the creek. While he was gone, she asked Bertie to tell the children the names of other plants she and Sally had seen. The children, who knew and accepted the use of herbs they found in the valley and on the mountainside, were happy to talk about them. They were deep into the discussion when James returned.

Will was with him, carrying his gun easily by the barrel.

"He helped me get it. Course I could've clumb the tree," James explained, proudly holding out a big hornet nest.

"Climbed," Charity corrected him automatically, before she realized what a hornet nest meant and cringed. "But we'll be stung." She half rose from the ground.

"Don't worry, it's an old nest. The hornets left it a long time ago," Will assured her.

Charity felt herself swelling inwardly with an absurd joy that Will was there. It seemed so long since they had done more than pass each other by. She decided to let the spelling lesson go for the present and asked Will and James to explain a little of hornets' habits to the children.

"The hornets keep adding to their nest year after year, then they leave it and start another one. Maybe it just gets too big for them." Will told them a little more about hornets and finished by reminding them that if they saw a hornet nest, they must leave it alone because if the hornets were still in it, they could be painfully stung. The children nodded, a couple of them making a frowning face that told Charity they were remembering how it hurt.

"Miss Charity," Bertie said. "Why don't you let me take the children for a walk and go home early? Isn't it too pert a day to go back to school?"

Surprised, Charity wondered if Bertie's own feelings for Dave were behind the obvious plan to leave Will alone here with her. But, looking at the children's exuberant faces, there was nothing she could do but agree. She almost wanted to run after the yelling, giggling children as they raced away, not waiting for Bertie, who didn't seem concerned.

There was no possibility of anything between Will and

herself as long as she couldn't be totally honest with him. And she couldn't betray her brother to someone who hated him so bitterly—someone who could turn Daniel in to the government for punishment and think that he would only be getting what he deserved. There was no way she could ever make Will see her brother as she did—a man of peace, fighting for what he believed in a war. Will could only see his friends, wounded and dying. Still, everything in her responded to just being with Will.

Will touched her arm. "Come up on the mountain with me. Let me show you what a day like this looks like from up there. We won't walk all the way up. There's a good place to cross the creek here. I know all the right stones."

Glad that he was talking and not waiting for an answer, Charity let him take her hand and guide her across the creek. They were laughing by the time she had leaped from one rock to the other, holding her skirts away from the water with one hand. She was deeply conscious of the pleasant firmness of his clasp, holding her hand a little more tightly as she made the final jump onto firm ground. He held it longer than needed to help her gain her balance, and she could feel the reluctance that matched her own when he finally opened his hand and let hers go. Neither felt the need to speak as they walked at a moderate pace up the slope.

❧

He stopped on an outcropping of rock a short way up the mountain. Not daring to look at her, he merely indicated the view below with a sweep of his hand. Wanting her to stay near, he was still almost relieved when she walked away to see the view from another angle.

How could he feel so close to this woman when he knew she was keeping a secret from him, when he was keeping the fact that he knew her secret from her? Not even a friendship could be built on such dishonesty; still, watching her, he admitted to himself that he loved her.

Yet, how could he let the man go free who had been the cause of the deaths of so many of his friends? Once again he could almost hear the sounds, smell the odors of that battlefield where they had no chance to win. Would it ever leave him? Would getting Charity's brother punished wash it from his mind? All he had to do was go into Asheville and tell his friend he knew where Daniel Morgan was, and it would all be over.

A sound from the bushes beside them jerked his attention back to the present. A bear suddenly reared up, eyeing Charity, who stood with her back to Will and to the bear. She had stopped to look at something on the ground, so absorbed that she didn't realize her danger.

Out of the corner of his eye, Will saw a half-grown cub up in a tree. Charity had come between the mama bear and the cub, and the angry bear was getting ready to charge.

Calling to Charity would only cause her to move and further frighten and anger the bear. The frantic mother would charge. He moved toward the bear, hoping to get her attention away from Charity and onto himself, but she had only one goal, to exterminate the thing that seemed to threaten her cub. She would hurt or kill Charity with a few swipes of her huge claws.

An angry growl from the bear caused Charity to jump and turn, and the bear moved toward her. Will knew there was only one thing he could do. He raced a few steps until he was diagonally across from the bear and positioned so that Charity wouldn't be hit by any of the scattering shot.

He trained the gun sights on the bear's chest, dragged the hammer back twice, and pulled the trigger. She went down in a pile of black fur. He saw the panic in Charity's face as she looked first toward him, then at the dead bear.

Without even looking at the bear again, he ran and caught Charity in his arms. "Charity, if you'd been hurt. . ." He didn't finish the sentence.

He felt Charity relax against him and they simply stood there holding each other for a few minutes, letting their closeness express the feelings neither of them could utter. Then Charity moved away to look at the bear.

"She was getting ready to attack you." Will felt that he had to explain to her why he'd killed the bear. "You were between her and her cub over there." He pointed to the frightened little bear up in his tree.

"Oh, she was only doing what she thought she had to do."

He watched tears fill her eyes and spill over her cheeks. He pulled her closer and put his hand on her head, snuggling it against his chest. For a moment that he was never to forget, she let him comfort her.

"But what about the little cub? Will it die, too?"

"From what I can see of it, it's old enough to feed itself and it should go into hibernation soon. It will probably stay up in the tree for at least tonight and I'll watch it for a few days, but I think it will be all right. But not happy."

She pulled herself away from him, and he reluctantly let her go.

"Will, I understand why you had to kill the bear and I

thank you for keeping her from hurting me, but. . .I wish it hadn't been necessary."

He didn't answer her directly. "Charity, I have to get the meat from the bear since it is dead. A lot of people in the valley will thank me for the meat. But I don't want you to stay while I do it. Can you get back to Birdsong Road by yourself?"

She nodded and turned to go off without saying anything further. A few feet away, she turned. "Will, please don't bring any of the meat to Aunt Nell."

He agreed not to, though ordinarily he would have, and he knew that Nell would have used the grease as base for some of her salves. He watched Charity as far as he could see her before he turned to the bear's carcass.

Before he brought out his knife to butcher the bear, Will checked out the position of the cub, glad that it had moved around to the other side of its tree and wouldn't watch him cutting up its mother. Grimacing, he thought of how other sons of the mountains would tease him for the emotions he had absorbed from Charity about the bear. Animals were killed for food or to protect yourself and sometimes for sport, but everything about them was used. Hardship for the animals was no more than a part of living.

But Charity's words stayed with him. *"She was only doing what she thought she had to do."*

The men who had killed each other in the war were only doing what they thought they had to do. The men on both sides.

He tried to turn his thoughts off as he worked at the bear's body, deliberately concentrating on what his hands were doing.

But his mind roared on to the idea he was trying to reject. All the men, including Daniel Morgan, were doing what they thought they had to do to protect whatever it was about their life that they loved.

He put the parts of the bear meat that he wanted to keep inside the skin and hung it from a branch of a tree to protect it from wolves while he went to get his horse to carry it back to disperse to families in the valley.

He was sure that the cub would stay in the tree long enough for him to check that Charity got home all right, get his horse, and come back before it came down to sniff at the spot where its mother died. Scoffing at himself, he still determined to bring back a shovel and bury the parts that he ordinarily would have left for the wolves.

sixteen

Charity hoped that no one saw her walking up Birdsong Road crying, not sure if she was crying for the bear, killed for trying to protect its young, or for Will and herself. How she longed to be back in Williamson County with her brother and mother, where Will Bowers would come to call and be judged by Daniel—now Peter—for the qualities he wanted in a husband for his sister. In that safe world before the war, Daniel would be like Will's older brother, not his enemy. . .not someone who must hide from him.

She jerked herself back to the present. That safe world was gone and she could never admit her love for Will, could never admit she loved him and still keep the secret she must keep to save her brother.

Passing the small overgrown path that led down to the house her brother had taken over, she longed to throw caution away and rush down there to tell him how she felt about Will, the way she'd told him about fancied attractions to boys a few years ago. But she didn't dare. Someone, even Will, might be watching her. Her need to be comforted by her brother might put his life in danger.

By the time she got home, she had control of herself and only answered Aunt Nell's concern about the obvious signs of her tears with the story of the bear.

"But, Aunt Nell, I've changed my mind about the all-day singing. I can control myself. Please, let's do it."

"Good girl. There's plenty of time to set it up this Sunday. Like I've said, these people will come out anytime to sing. It's late in the year. We used to have the all-day singing in the summer, but that's no matter. With Daniel here, they'll come. They'll come."

Charity left it at that. Whatever was needed to get the people together for the song meeting was done by Aunt Nell and whoever she got to help.

There was a definite chill in the air on Sunday and clouds that threatened to rain any minute. "We'll just have to be inside," Aunt Nell said, determinedly. "They'll come."

"What about the dinner on the grounds?" Uncle Doc asked.

"Well. . .the Lord will provide. Maybe the sun will come out." Aunt Nell went on, wrapping a clean towel around a cake. "We'll eat somewhere just like we'll sing somewhere. I just wish that Johnny and Vern hadn't split up over the war. They did about the best harmonizing that ever happened around here. How I'd love to hear it again. You have the chicken and dumplings, Charity? Well, let's go. Show the rest of the valley that the singing's still on."

Once they were on Birdsong Road, they were joined by other neighbors carrying food. Someone started humming a song Charity didn't recognize, and the pace of the group picked up as others joined in. They came to the church already in a singing mood.

Daniel and Joshua were standing at the front of the church, and several people were sitting inside talking. Bethany had cajoled them into putting up a long board on sawhorses out in the churchyard in front, and Tabitha Ballard and Virgie Smith were directing the food to be placed on it. They stayed out to watch that no bugs or squirrels came near the food while the rest of the group went on into the church.

"Don't look now," Aunt Nell whispered to Charity as they walked in, "but Johnny Myers is on the front row and Vern Rogers on the back. Those two men couldn't stay away, but they're deliberately leaving as many rows of seats between them as possible."

Charity, ignoring her admonition not to look, identified the two men, then caught herself looking for Will, not sure if she was hoping he would be there or that he wouldn't. What if he somehow recognized Daniel? She reminded herself to remember to call him Peter. Just as Joshua stepped forward to open with prayer, she saw Will slip in and sit down in the back on the other end of the seat where Vern sat. Before she quickly turned her gaze back to the front, she saw Vern scowl at Will.

≈

Will was aware of Vern's frown and ignored it. He was here for one thing, to watch Daniel Morgan. Daniel Morgan, no matter what he chose to call himself now. Will felt like he hadn't slept at all since he'd killed the bear threatening Charity. He had checked on the cub two days in a row and on the second day had found it gone. He was reasonably sure it could live on its own.

It wasn't the cub that was bothering him and he knew it. It was Charity. Coming back from a hopeless war to a hopeless love was unfair. Even if Charity returned his love, they couldn't do anything about it with the secret of Daniel Morgan between them. Resentment toward Daniel flooded his mind and kept him from hearing Joshua's prayer.

Seeing Mattie slip into the last row of the women's side only made him feel angrier. How could an old mountain woman like her make him feel guilty for not agreeing that the men Daniel Morgan had caused to die deserved revenge? She'd had a rough life, but she'd never watched friends shot down like animals.

He was brought back by Daniel Morgan stepping down close to the congregation and surprising everyone by sounding out the happy Christmas song, "Joy to the World." After a moment of amazement, the congregation moved into the spirit of the song and filled the church with the delight of the animated chorus.

After two more songs, Joshua Holt gave a short sermon that Will tried not to hear, refusing the words of forgiveness and peace that Joshua seemed almost to be directing toward him, then wondering briefly if everyone in there felt the same way.

He looked at Dave, sitting on the women's side with Bertie and Sally. Dave had never adequately explained Charity's kidnapping, and Will had stopped asking after he found out who Charity's brother was. The answer must have had something to do with Daniel Morgan.

After more songs and a closing prayer, the congregation filed outside for their noontime dinner, murmuring thanks that the sun had come out, some of them still carefully staying only with those whose war sympathies agreed with theirs, even as they filled their plates and found a place to eat.

Will slipped in back of the church, where the horses were tied or left free to graze if their owners knew they would stay. He gathered up his horse's reins and guided him out into the trees, not wanting to go past the people eating and determined not to eat with them. He might be wavering about turning Daniel Morgan in, but he didn't trust himself to be close to him. And he certainly wasn't going to watch Charity hurt while trying not to show that Peter Matthews was anything more to her than the new songmaster.

He rode back out to the place where he'd killed the bear to check on the cub one last time. It was still nowhere around, and he was sure it had gone back to whatever cave it had spent a winter in with its mother. It would come out in the spring a young adult.

Will had brought a change of clothes in his saddlebag with the idea of possibly riding out for Asheville, but something took him back to the church. He didn't question that it was Charity who led him back. An afternoon near her was too tempting to resist.

They had already finished eating and were sitting around on the grass or on quilts when he got back. He walked around to the front of the church, where Charity was sitting with Bertie and Sally. Bertie waved to him, seeming to invite him over, but he pretended he didn't see her. He couldn't sit beside Charity while he was considering whether or not to inform on her brother. He stayed at the edges of the crowd but placed himself where he could see her.

Gus Yates had a banjo and Daniel asked him to play a few songs for them. He started with "Amazing Grace," and the group started singing without being directed. Soon they were mixing church songs with old folk songs that everyone knew. Johnny Myers and Vern Rogers were sitting closer to each other than in the church. Close enough to hear each other's voices.

Daniel seemed to be watching them. Will couldn't believe it when he suddenly asked the two to come up and sing together.

For a long moment, there was a silence as everyone there seemed to project their own tension. Then Johnny stood up and walked forward, not looking at Vern. He started singing, "Deep river; my home is over Jordan." After a few bars, Vern joined in from where he sat. Their voices blended as they used to do when they stood head to head and sang together. At the end of the song, Daniel invited them with a gesture to sing another.

In the middle of "On Jordan's Stormy Banks I Stand," Vern rose and went up to stand beside Johnny. They finished the song together.

Will saw tears on the faces of some of the women in the group. Even his father was looking out into the trees on the mountain, seeming to try to control his expression.

Will turned away and walked back to his horse. He mounted and turned the horse's head toward the mountain, his mind in a turmoil. This Daniel Morgan who had caused him so much pain had brought a healing to the valley. How could he take him away from his neighbors? What was the answer?

Words ran through his mind, deafening him: Mattie's "since they're in a place where there's no fighting, maybe they'd rather have forgiveness than revenge"; Charity's "she was only doing what she had to do to protect her cub."

Daniel Morgan had done what he thought he had to do. He, Will Bowers, had done what he thought he had to do. Daniel Morgan had turned to the healing of music; where could he find healing? In revenge or in forgiving? In taking away someone who had brought some peace to the valley, or in giving them a gift that they would never know about by keeping quiet?

He had come to the waterfall on Falling Water Creek. He got off his horse and let him wander off to graze. Afternoon sun streaked along the stream and flashed off the falling water. Feeling a closeness to the God who created the sun and the water, Will moved nearer. "What, God? What should I do?"

Then, on an impulse he didn't understand, he took his shirt off and lifted his arms toward the sky. Feeling the soft touch of the spray from the waterfall, almost like a gentle hand, he dropped to his knees. "Help me, please, God. Help me."

seventeen

"You're coming home with us after the singing," Bethany said. "Peter will be there and there will just be you and Dad and Nell, so we can be relaxed."

Charity smiled. She knew that Bethany was telling her that they were giving her a chance to be with Daniel without having to pretend she didn't know him.

Inside Bethany's house, Charity could see that Bethany had used all her sewing skill to make cheerful curtains and table covers for her new home. Charity found herself thinking of how she would decorate a home at some future time, without allowing herself to consider who might share it with her. Certainly it wouldn't be Will Bowers.

A wooden porch ran the length of the house and, without conscious direction, they all found seats either on chairs brought out from the house or on the floor. Charity sat by Daniel on the edge of the porch, reveling in the chance to rest in the circle of his arm. Too well fed at the singing to want more than cold dandelion root tea, they watched the feathery sunset clouds over the mountains in contented silence.

Daniel broke the silence as the rose-flamed clouds faded into lavender. "Little sister, I saw a tall, handsome man looking at you today. Has he asked Doc if he can court you?"

Charity felt his arm tighten about her shoulders as he looked away; she knew his thoughts. It should be him who gave Will permission to court her.

The silence on the porch had suddenly lost its easy comfort. She could feel Daniel's concerned gaze on her, but she couldn't meet his eyes.

"What is it, Charity? Tell me." His voice held the tone she remembered when her mother had sent her to him after she had broken a rule of the house. It meant she must respond. But she was no longer a child. She stubbornly looked away.

"I believe you should tell him about Will, Charity. For his protection, if nothing else. Or do you want me to tell him?"

"I. . .yes, please, Aunt Nell."

"Will Bowers is a danger to you, Daniel—"

"Peter, please," he interrupted.

"Will is a danger to Daniel Morgan, if he finds out who you are."

"Used to be," Daniel insisted.

"He was in a Union company. He thinks that your. . . activity. . .may have made an ambush possible. A lot of his friends. . .were killed. He's very bitter. I think he would turn you in if he knew."

Daniel sat staring into the darkening sky for what seemed to Charity to be an eternity. Then he took his arm from her shoulder and stood up, turning to face the group on the porch.

"I will go to him. I will tell him."

"Peter, you can't. Think of your work here in the valley." Joshua sounded shattered.

"Joshua, I want to work with you here in Falling Water

Valley for the rest of my life, and I know that making my true name known to everyone here might undo anything I've managed to do in the short time I've been here. But I can't do any good work knowing that my presence here is causing one man to nurse old angers. I have to ask Will Bowers for forgiveness. He can decide whether to forgive me or turn me in. But I must ask. I'll go to him tomorrow."

Charity shivered. She wasn't sure if the breeze had chilled or the cold came from inside her. *Winter's coming on*, she thought, wishing Daniel would come sit beside her again.

There was a long silence as each of them thought their own thoughts in the gathering darkness.

&

"Charity, I know you want to know what happened when Peter went to see Will." Charity looked up from her desk in surprise as Aunt Nell walked briskly into the schoolroom, her wool shawl pulled tight against the cold air outside.

"I haven't been able to think of anything else today. Is this why you came down to the school?"

"Yes. I. . .there are things I think you need to know. I could hardly wait until the children left."

Charity felt her face tighten. "Will refused? Oh, Aunt Nell is he going to. . .?"

"He wasn't there. Annie said he rode into Asheville yesterday."

"Then Daniel. . .Peter. . .hasn't talked to him at all? That's a relief, Aunt Nell. Why did you say you're worried?"

"Mattie came to see Bethany this morning. After seeing how well our neighbors responded to Daniel yesterday, she decided that she needed to warn us. Will knows who Daniel really is. One of his old company lives in Asheville. He's been talking to someone who knows a bounty hunter and gave him such a good description that he recognized him." She sighed. "We must have been too quick to believe what we wanted to, not to realize that someone would recognize Daniel. . .maybe, if I'd done something about that red hair. . . Will knows how to contact the bounty hunter."

For a long moment Charity stared out the door at the leaves twisting about in the blustering gusts. Suddenly she felt colder than the weather outside.

"He's gone to turn Daniel in. Daniel has to get out of the valley."

Aunt Nell shook her head. "Daniel won't go. He isn't going to run anymore."

"Oh, Aunt Nell, he has to. I've got to talk to him. I'm going over to his house. It's too late now to keep pretending I'm not his sister."

Aunt Nell didn't argue. "Take my horse. I'll walk home."

"Oh, will you be sure Wilder is in before you close the door? I'm still keeping him inside at night."

"Of course. Go on, honey."

Charity hardly felt the wind as she rode up to the cabin where Daniel was staying. She slid off the horse and ran to the door, giving it a couple of hard knocks.

Daniel opened it immediately. He grinned down at her. "I knew when I heard the banging on the door that it was you. You never could wait for a ladylike knock. Come on in, Charity. I'm sorry I only have two hard chairs, but let's sit in them. I suppose you want to talk."

Charity looked at him for a moment without speaking. How could he look so sure of himself when Will might at that moment be telling some money-hungry bounty hunter just where to find him? She was too restless to sit in the chair he pulled from a rough wooden table. That and a bed seemed to be the only furniture in the cabin. A picture of the polished secretary desk in his office on the farm flowed through her mind. She forced it out to let the words she needed take its place.

"I do want to talk. You have to leave, Daniel. You must." She paced from window to door and back again.

He shook his head, drawing her close under his arm as he walked with her. "No, my dearest sister, I won't leave."

"Why, Daniel? You can't just stay here and let Will bring men in to take you."

Daniel stopped still, forcing Charity to stand. He put both hands on her shoulders, turning her to face him.

"Charity, this valley is a gift God has given to me. A place to make some recompense for the work I had to do in the war. If the short time I've been here is the limit of that gift, then I'll accept that. But I won't run anymore. I won't spend more time with that unruly group of men who are still using the war to make excuses for their lawlessness and I won't leave my South. I was fighting for it. If I leave it now, what was I fighting for?"

"I don't care, Daniel. I only know that I can't bear to lose you, too."

"Yes, you can, Charity Charlotte Morgan. You're a strong person and you can bear what you need to bear."

Charity forced a shadow of a smile. "Are you going to make me fill up my slate with 'I Can Learn to Bear It'?"

He laughed, obviously remembering with her a time

back in Williamson County. "No, I believe that was 'I can learn to embroider my sampler'. Learning to take what life hands out is harder. Now I was getting ready to eat a bowl of cornbread and milk. I'll share it with you."

"That's it, Daniel? That's all you're having for supper?"

"I found over the past few years that it doesn't take a lot of food to keep a body going. Now if you'll just sit your body down here," he easily lifted the two chairs and placed them at the table, "I'll serve you this delicious meal."

Charity sat down thinking that she couldn't force even the softness of bread and milk past her fear-tightened throat, but she discovered a comfort in the familiar feeling of sitting again at a table with Daniel. She seemed to have a heightened sense of taste as she ate.

"Daniel?"

"Yes, little sister."

"About doing the sewing sampler. I talked Miss Simpson into doing it for me."

He grinned at her. "I know. She sent me the account for doing it along with her other sewing."

"Oh, Daniel, I'm sorry. Sorry, I tried to fool you and Mama. If we could go back—" Charity felt all her agitation melt into tears. She put her spoon in the bowl, laid her head on Daniel's shoulder, and sobbed. He simply held her close until she had cried it out and drew back. Then he stood up.

"You're officially forgiven, Charity. And now you must leave. No matter what happens, I'm glad we've had this short time together."

"Daniel, how can you be so calm, so sure?"

"It isn't just that I refuse to run for the rest of my life,

Charity. I have faith in God. I also have faith in your Will."

"My Will?"

"I've seen how he looks at you, Charity. I've seen your face when he's near. And, because I could see him wanting to court you and you wanting to be courted, I talked with Nell and Dr. Andrews about him. He's a fine young man and if we were at home, I would approve of you marrying him. And I believe he can do what is best for everyone. Now, be sure no one is about before you go out my door. We don't want to cause gossip about the schoolmarm."

Charity tried to respond to his last light remark, failed, and kissed his cheek before leaving. She wished she could feel as certain that everything would turn out right as Daniel did, but she couldn't. Daniel hadn't heard Will's bitter declarations.

❧

Will had told his parents that he might ride into Asheville to see his old friend. He left the waterfall behind and rode until dark, then lay down to sleep on a cleared area somewhere between the valley and Asheville. He rode into Asheville the next day and went directly to the boarding-house where Rance Hunt lived.

"I'm sorry I can't offer you anything but water," Rance said, motioning Will to a chair. "The landlady takes everything away after I eat. To keep the bugs down, she says."

"It's all right, Rance. I don't want anything." As he spoke, Will realized that he couldn't remember when he last ate. He didn't think he'd eaten anything at the dinner and singing. But he was truthful when he said he didn't want anything.

"I know. What you want is news about Daniel Morgan.

Well, it isn't good. He's gone."

"He's gone?"

"That's right. Gone. Got away. To Canada."

"Rance, what are you saying? How do you know?"

"Bounty hunter told me. He came by and said just stop writing letters. Old Morgan has been seen several times in Canada. He tore out of here like greased lightning and there's nothing we can do about it. He's safe as he can be up there."

Will caught his breath. Could it be true that Peter Matthews was just what he said he was? That Daniel Morgan was someone else who had eluded all his hunters and made it to Canada? He wanted to believe it. He could fight for Charity's love if Peter was just a friend. He would spend the rest of his life fighting for her love if he needed to. He could. . .

He couldn't fool himself. The exceptionally tall red-headed man with a limp who made Charity's face light up was her brother. Someone else had been seen in Canada— someone who probably hadn't had anything to do with the late war.

Now was the time. He could tell Rance Hunt where Daniel Morgan really was and see him dragged off within days. He could see his dead companions avenged, or he could see Peter Matthews bringing something to the valley. Who was right, Mattie or Rance?

Then, he knew. Suddenly he knew as well as if he had never questioned. Back on Falling Water Creek he'd asked God to help him decide, and his prayer had been answered.

He stood up. "I need to go now, Rance. I'll come back to see you later. I'll come back often."

eighteen

"It seems like this kind of weather just makes babies decide to come," Aunt Nell said, taking her heavy cloak off the hook.

"Maybe it's a little boy who can't wait to throw snowballs," Uncle Doc said, grinning. "I'm going with you. One person shouldn't be out alone in this. You can get lost in a blizzard like this no matter that you know this valley like your own face. I'll saddle the horses."

"I won't argue one mite. I'll be glad to have you. And I may need you to help me birth this one. Sarah Baldwin's so small. Charity, we'll probably be gone all day. I'm just glad that this storm started in the night so you weren't in school."

"So am I," Charity answered. "I wouldn't want any of my children to be out in this."

"I'm sorry we have to go. I know that it isn't easy for you to be alone now. But, at least, maybe the snow will keep Will from coming home from Asheville and maybe Daniel will get some kind of good sense if he has extra time to think about it. I don't want to see him leave the valley when Joshua needs his help so badly, but getting hauled away by bounty hunters won't be any different."

"He won't change his mind, Aunt Nell. He's determined to take a stand here. I sort of understand, but not really. I don't think I can bear to lose him again."

"We can only pray," Aunt Nell said, giving Charity a quick hug. "We'll be back as soon as we can."

She hurried out, her expression showing that she was already mentally with her patient, in spite of her concern for Daniel.

Charity watched them disappear into the shimmering white cloud that surrounded the cabin; then, feeling the cold coming around the edges of the window, she moved over to stand by the fireplace. Somehow the heat from the fire didn't seem to dissipate the chill that was wrapping her bones.

If Will had already turned Daniel in, there was nothing that would keep the bounty hunters away. No storm. Nothing.

She moved away from the fireplace, wandered into her room, came back again. She wished she had brought Wilder home with her from the school. Perhaps his soft body would warm hers. And would he be all right there alone? After all, there was no fire in the school fireplace. She sat down and then immediately stood up.

She couldn't spend this day shut up alone in the house, imagining what might be going on at Daniel's house. She wanted to go see if he was all right, but she didn't dare. Some mental fragment from her childhood kept her from letting him know that she would do something so foolish as to go out in this storm. She almost giggled, thinking that he might make her stand in the corner for a half hour. But nothing funny stayed with her today. She let her thoughts go back to rescuing Wilder. She really was concerned about him.

Making a sudden decision, she went into the other room.

Aunt Nell was wearing her heavy brogans, but she had another pair and she wouldn't mind Charity searching for them and wearing them. Charity didn't let herself consider how much Aunt Nell might mind her going out in the storm. She couldn't stay inside any longer.

She found the piece of slate they used to communicate with each other and chalked the words, "Back in a little bit." Best not to mention what she planned.

The heavy shoes were too big, but she ignored that. She got her winter cloak out of her room and tied a wool knit scarf about her head and throat.

The door opened easily, letting snow blow in. The wet flakes felt good to Charity's flushed face. It was harder to pull the door closed, but she succeeded and turned to face the wind. It was stronger than she had expected, but the snow wasn't deeper than the tops of her shoes and she could protect her face by pulling her scarf across it.

She felt exhilarated. The twisting snow was weaving a world of its own, far away from her fretful thoughts. She could lose herself in the beauty swirling around her and trimming the trees and bushes.

She found Birdsong Road without any trouble and followed it. It was awhile before she began to really feel the chill. It was almost from one minute to the next that she realized that both her feet and hands were wet and freezing.

She decided to turn off on the lane going down to Daniel's cabin. It would be better to let him fuss at her than to stay out in this. And she would know if he was still there and not taken by a bounty hunter. She only realized that she had passed the lane without seeing it when the snow thinned suddenly and she saw the welcome dim outlines of the school. A fire in the fireplace would be welcome, too.

She could hear Wilder's raucous voice complaining inside while she spent several minutes kicking the snow away and shoving against the door. When it finally gave, it almost hit Wilder, who showed his appreciation of her rescue by climbing her cloak and clinging to her shoulder.

"Just give me a few minutes to build a fire, Wilder, and we'll both warm up."

He clambered about her feet while she took matches out of a niche in the logs and touched one to the kindling she laid each afternoon before leaving school. In a few minutes little flashes of flame hopped in and out of the wood, turning quickly into a leaping fire.

She took Wilder over to sit on one of the student's benches, cuddling him inside her cloak. As the room warmed and he drowsed off against her arm, she felt herself growing sleepy. Moving carefully so as to not disturb him, she slipped down onto the bench and went to sleep.

She woke from a confused dream that left drifting memories of Williamson County, though she couldn't remember why. The fire had died down and the room was becoming chilly again. There was a dimness in the air that wasn't quite night, but a startling warning that it was coming on.

She jumped up, forgetting about Wilder until he bellowed his annoyance at her as he hit the floor.

"Come on, Wilder," she said, picking him up. "It's past time to go home. And it's still snowing."

She poked and stirred the fire to make sure it was out and, holding Wilder under her cloak, hurried out. Her first step took her into snow up to her knee. Gasping at the icy stuff sliding into her shoe, she lifted her foot back to the stone step and watched in dismay as the too-large shoe stayed buried in the snow.

She stood on one foot, watching a horse forming through the angling snow and wondering if the shock of the snow was giving her hallucinations. But the horse came closer, and she could see that there was a man on it.

"Maybe it's my white knight," she murmured to Wilder, remembering Miss Jane's stories of the days of chivalry. Then she could see that it was Will. "No. Not now. Not today."

Wild thoughts ran through her mind. *Run to warn Daniel. He could get away on a day like this and they might trail him, but they couldn't find him once he got into the mountains. Mattie could hide him.* Then reality hit her. She was standing on one freezing foot while her shoe filled up with snow and Will, on a horse, was between her and Daniel.

Will swung down and waded through the snow toward her. "I was past the lane when I saw smoke and some sparks coming from the school chimney."

"I was making sure the fire was out." How could they be having such an ordinary conversation when she wanted to scream at him that she knew what he was doing to Daniel? How could she want to walk into his arms at the same time? She could almost feel his warmth.

"You. . .where's your shoe?"

"Down there." She indicated the hollow in the snow.

Something in Will's eyes told her he wanted to laugh but didn't dare. He slid his arm into the snow and brought up

Aunt Nell's brogan, filled with snow. He shook as much of the snow out as he could and set it down beside her.

"Why are you down here? Did the storm catch you in school? Are there any children in there?"

"No. I came down to get Wilder."

"You did? How could you? You walked down? Miss Nell let you?"

"The snow wasn't so deep then. Wilder and I went to sleep. Aunt Nell and Uncle Doc went to a baby birthing. I left them a note."

He frowned. "Well, the snow is plenty deep now."

"I know." She looked in despair at her shoe and once again she had an impression of suppressed laughter. In fact, everything about Will seemed somehow too cheerful for the stormy day. Maybe getting even with Daniel was satisfying to him.

"Do you want to put that shoe back on?"

She looked at the shoe and shuddered. There was no good decision to make. Without answering, she shoved her foot into the cold mass, trying desperately not to show her discomfort.

"You can't walk back. You'll ride with me."

She wanted to refuse his high-handed offer, but she knew that arguing would be pure foolishness. Her foot would be frozen before she could walk back to any place of warmth.

He brought his horse up to the step and started to help her into the saddle. Before he could touch her, she handed a splayed out, clawing Wilder to him. While he was trying to cope with the cat, she swung herself into the saddle, almost losing the shoe again. But there was a limit to how much help she would accept from him.

He caught the bridle and shoved Wilder back into her hands. As she hid the angry cat under her cloak, he swung up behind her and reached around her to guide the horse. This was closer than she had planned, but somehow it felt safe and comforting. She wouldn't allow herself to feel anything more. They rode without talking.

Suddenly he guided the reluctant horse off Birdsong Road and into a barely outlined lane. Charity stiffened. It had to be the lane leading down to Daniel.

Nebulous plans shot through her mind, none of them possible, all of them taking up too much time. They must be getting close to Daniel's cabin. There was only one thing she could do. For Daniel, she would beg.

She turned toward Will. "I know you know who Daniel is. Please don't—"

But Will had already stopped the horse and dismounted. She wasn't sure he had even heard her. If he had, he didn't respond as he reached for her. She was too despondent to fight him. Holding Wilder, she let him help her down, feeling the strength of his arms for the last time.

Daniel stood in the door when they turned, beckoning them into the warmth of the room behind him. He got their outdoor clothes off, pulled his two chairs up close to the fireplace, and brought them mugs of hot chamomile tea before any of the three had much to say. Charity briefly explained what happened to her shoe.

Then Daniel leaned against the log mantel. "Are you warm enough to talk now?"

Charity looked at him in admiration. He didn't know if Will already had bounty hunters following him, but he had cared for them with dignity and now was opening the necessary talk with Will. And he was facing whatever Will might choose to do.

Charity could do no less. "I believe we are, Daniel."

Will didn't respond to the name.

"Yes, Will," Daniel said. "She is calling me by my right name. Daniel Morgan, Confederate spy." He walked over and placed both hands on Charity's shoulders. "I am Charity's brother. And I am in your hands. I can ask your forgiveness, but I can't live here in hiding, knowing that I'm forcing you to let your anger and bitterness grow. We will do whatever will ease your mind."

Will stood and faced them. He took in a deep breath, and Charity felt that she would never breathe again.

"Daniel Morgan, I'm respectfully asking your permission to call on your sister."

nineteen

Charity slipped off Rainbow's back and dropped the reins. The horse, at home at the falls of Falling Water Creek, immediately walked off toward the heaviest growth of grass and started grazing, seeming to enjoy the clover blossoms as much as the grass.

Charity watched her idly for a while, hearing the raucous warning of a nearby blue jay and a chickadee farther back in the trees. It was a few minutes before she noticed a group of hummingbirds fluttering in and out of a tangle of showy purple rhododendron. She stood close enough to the waterfall to enjoy the coolness of the spray against the heat of the August day. Wanting to be even closer, she sat in the shallow depression of a large rock on the edge of the creek. She briefly thought of taking off her shoes and letting the chilly water caress her feet but decided not to after considering the gravel surrounding the rock.

She needed the time to ease off from the happy bustle of getting ready for her wedding; time to think about all the things that had happened since she came into Falling Water Valley, the unfolding events since Will and Daniel had made peace with each other, and Daniel's effect on the rest of the valley residents.

She thought back to her visit to Daniel's cabin after the snowstorm had stopped and the snow had melted. Daniel had been sitting beside his only window, totally engrossed in matching off-shaped pieces of wood. He called out "Come in" when she knocked, without coming to the door.

"Good. It's you," he said, looking up from the thin slabs of wood he held in his lap. "Just come on in. There's some real coffee on the stove if you want. Well, almost real. It's a mixture. Makes the coffee last longer. I can't turn loose of this right now." He indicated the wood he was holding, which seemed strangely important to him.

"You didn't even look to see who it was before you asked me to come in," Charity chided. "I know you're feeling good about Will, but that doesn't mean someone else may not want to. . .to hurt you."

Daniel grinned. "I suppose I'm the only one feeling good about Will, of course. I did give permission for him to court my little sister. Somehow I thought you'd want me to."

Charity answered his grin, but stuck to her concern, ignoring the invitation to coffee. "You still didn't even ask who was there before you invited me in. I could have been anybody. And you don't even have the bolt drawn on your door."

"Sweetheart, if someone wants to get even with me, I can't stop them unless I go live in the wilderness, and I got enough of that in the short time I spent with the outliers. Living isn't worth what I saw them doing to people. And if I can't bring these good people here to accept me, I can't do it anywhere."

He stopped and stared at his hands, holding the wood tightly for several minutes while Charity waited silently.

"Charity, I know I'm going to spend the rest of my life regretting the war and a lot of my part in it, but I did what I felt I had to do for my beliefs. Now, I refuse to spend the rest of my life fighting it over and over again. I'm going to go back to my real name and I'm going to make a life here or let it go. This," he once again indicated the woods he held tightly, "is a part of my plan for that."

"What is it?" She walked closer and concentrated intently on the structure, still unable to identify it.

"You've seen me play back in Tennessee. It's a dulcimer."

Charity looked more closely. "But the dulcimer you played there was a beautiful, soft, curved. . ." She stopped talking and let her hands describe the shape in the air. "That's just a square—well, a rectangle."

"I know. I don't have all the tools here to make a more gracious one. But this will make music. Samuel Bowers cut the wood thin for me with his froe. By the way, he and Annie seem to be very happy about Will's choice."

He smiled at her and she returned it. "I was so scared when I knew Will had told them about you."

Daniel nodded. "He talked to me about it first. He hadn't told them what was causing him so much anguish, but they'd sensed it and were just glad to know he'd found his peace, as well as finding you. They, and Dave, know that I will tell everyone who I am and ask for their forgiveness. This," he indicated the partially finished instrument, "is a part of my plan for doing that. This valley loves music. We know it has begun to bring them together."

Not wanting to think about what might happen when Daniel told his real identity, Charity turned back to the wood in his hand. "Why are you holding it like that?"

"I just glued these pieces together. I've got some bricks to hold them together for several days while the glue dries good, but I want to make sure they're in place for now.

Aunt Nell had a piece of dried animal skin and she boiled it down into glue for me. I decided not to ask her what kind of animal it was."

Charity wrinkled her nose. "I thought I caught a whiff of something cooking that I didn't recognize. She had a fire going outside, thank goodness. But, are you taking the dulcimer to church?"

He shook his head. "Grant Williams has a fiddle he hasn't played in public since before the war. He wants to play again. I thought maybe our schoolmarm might let us have a musical down at the school some evening."

"Taking the sun, are you?"

Charity jumped at the sound of the harsh voice coming from behind her. She had been so caught up in memories that she hadn't heard Mattie come up. She wondered, as she had before, how such a large woman could move so silently. There had been a time when Mattie's sudden appearance would have disturbed her. But over the months she had learned of her friendship with Bethany and her wise and helpful words to Will when he was torn about Daniel, and she had much to be grateful to Mattie for. Charity had been with her enough to understand and respect the sense of freedom and closeness to God that Mattie found in her life alone on the mountain.

She grinned up at Mattie, honestly glad to see her. "You willing to share some of your sunshine and water with me?"

Mattie grinned back. "It's free to everybody. You runnin' away from all the falderal of the wedding?"

Charity nodded. "I needed some time away. Some time alone just to think about my happiness."

"Then I'll leave you thanking God for it."

"You don't have to leave, Mattie."

"I came here to go into my cave behind the waterfall. Not mine by law really. But it means a lot to me. Want to go in with me?"

Charity looked at the water, now diminished because of the dry summer, dancing down from a massive rock and shook her head. "It means a lot to me too. But, not now, Mattie. I'm too comfortable to move."

Mattie nodded, seeming to understand more than Charity had said. With no more need for words, she walked over and disappeared into an opening in the rock behind the waterfall.

Charity let her mind drift back to the musical at the school, where Daniel had stood up and told the people who he was and asked their forgiveness and acceptance.

She had let school out early on a sunny April Friday. It would soon be time for the boys and girls to help with the spring planting and cleaning at home, and it was the last day they would have school. They would do a short program in the evening before the musical to show their parents and neighbors what they had accomplished during the school year.

"Miss Charity, let me take the children out to find decorations for the school," Bertie offered.

Charity agreed, glad to see the overexcited children flocking around Bertie. James, the tallest of the children, stayed to help her attach a sheet, borrowed from Aunt Nell, across the front of the school to be a curtain for their play.

By the time they had folded and sewn the sheet on a rope nailed to the log walls, the children were back. Some of them held arms full of dogwood branches, bearing the greenish white of still unopened buds, while Bertie was carefully carrying two twigs with graceful white blossoms of silver bell hanging from them. Two of the girls clutched short stems of violets and spring beauty, already wilting.

Charity received it all with delighted thanks and helped them place everything about the schoolroom. After they had decorated, she led them through one last practice of the simple play they had planned and written together. Then she sent them home to come back with their families in the evening.

Will came early and helped her place lanterns requisitioned from the Bowerses and Andrewses to light up the "stage," now set up with Charity's desk and two benches for the play that would start the evening.

Neighbors soon came in with lanterns of their own, which they placed about the schoolroom. As they found seats, many of the mothers delighted their children with compliments for the decorations. In the rather dim light of the lanterns, the fast-fading greenery still looked festive.

After Joshua's opening prayer, Charity pulled the hanging sheet back and watched with quiet pride as her students held their make-believe class. They had correctly thought that the audience would get a laugh from having little Sally play the teacher, and she put her "students" through their paces "right smartly," creating a happy mood that lasted for the rest of the evening.

After James had pulled the "curtain" to end the show and the laughter and pride of the audience had turned into applause, Sally easily went to Dave's side. He swept her into his arms for a moment before seating her between himself and her mother. James, without being told, pulled the sheet back to one side to make room for the musicians.

Now Charity sat down beside Will, who surreptitiously held her hand tightly, while they watched Daniel with his dulcimer and Grant, carrying his fiddle, move to the front where Sally had led her students. Trying to keep her own face impassive, Charity looked around at Uncle Doc and Aunt Nell, Joshua and Bethany, Samuel and Annie Bowers. Reading the anxiety in the tense posture of each of them, she knew that they were as frightened as she was.

She knew the neighbors would enjoy and respond to the music, but, afterwards, what would they do to Daniel when he stood before them as Daniel Morgan, not Peter Matthews? Would they be able to give him the forgiveness he asked for?

Daniel and Grant played old songs, songs brought over from the old world by their ancestors. The audience listened and often sang with them, enjoying ballads of broken love and nonsense songs of repeated absurd sounds.

Caleb Grainger, the seventy-year-old storyteller of the valley, caught up in the festive atmosphere, interrupted to tell a long story of the legendary hero, Jack. It was obviously a favorite with the audience from days before the war, and they joined in with the frequent repetitions of "and Jack traveled on," as told by their grandfathers and great-grandfathers.

Finally, the music stopped, Grant sat down to enthusiastic clapping and Daniel stood there alone. He waited quietly for the applause to die down, then started to talk. Clutching Will's hand tightly, Charity watched his face intensely for any sign that there might be anxiety under the calm expression. Seeing none, she knew that Daniel, secure in his faith and nearness to his God, was ready for whatever might happen.

He took a short step toward the audience. "I hope you have enjoyed the music tonight. I hope you have received consolation and spiritual closeness to our God from the music we have shared at church since I came to your beautiful valley. Because you are going to decide tonight if I am to become a real part of this valley where you have made me feel at home for the past few months."

He stopped and drew in a deep breath, while the audience seemed so quiet as to be holding theirs, waiting for whatever he might be going to add. The silence, itself, showed their expectation of something important.

"I am a fugitive. I came here to hide. But I have learned that hiding is not going to let me be what I want to be to you and what I want you to be to me. I thank those of you who have known who I am and have been a refuge for me, but now I must tell you. I am Daniel Morgan, Nell's nephew and Charity's brother. And, yes, the Confederate spy. The Union men still hunt me, though the war is over. I've received forgiveness and peace from our God; now I ask yours for being among you without telling you who I am. But if you wish, now you may tell them where I am. I am at your mercy."

There was an excitement running through the crowd. Someone briefly clapped. Carl Dietz shouted, "Rah. You can stay here forever."

Then there was silence again, while the neighbors looked at each other, trying to understand what having this former spy with them might foretell.

Without speaking, Clyde McMillan rose and walked

out, his face an angry mask. Bertie McMillan watched him go, then stood up, holding Sally's hand. "My father-in-law can't seem to ever get the forgiving spirit I pray for him. But he's a God-fearing man. He won't harm you, Mr. Morgan. And I reckon as many of us as can will want you here for the singing and for our Nell. I'll pray for you. I'll pray for us all."

She sat down, her face flushed and looking scared from her uncharacteristic public speech. Charity almost smiled to see Dave reach across Sally to catch and hold her hand.

The others went into a cacophony of whispered and hushed comments and questions. Dave Bradley ended it by coming up to stand by Daniel.

"Neighbors," he addressed the crowd, "some of you know, some don't, that I was a Union spy. Some of you may still want to take a gun to me for that. I hope not. But, like Daniel, I want you to know. Now I have one question for Daniel, then I want to shake his hand and ask him to stay. Daniel Morgan, you've asked forgiveness from this valley. But the war is over and we're one country again. Are you going to ask pardon from our government and say you believe in the United States of America? Will you take the oath of allegiance to our government?"

"Yes, I will try," Daniel replied, his face showing his doubt that it would be granted. He ignored a low murmur of disapproval from someone in the back. "Now, let the two of us, who would have met each other with bullets before, shake hands."

Afterwards, Dave had taken some of the crowd's attention with the news that he and Bertie were getting married. "You're all invited to this wedding, which will be as soon as

Sally gets her new dress from Asheville."

After the general relieved laughter had died down, the crowd gathered up their lanterns and left in thoughtful silence. Charity noticed that as they walked into the night, they moved in tight groups of those with the same sympathies, as though still reluctant, or afraid, to give up their prejudices.

Three days later, Charity was visiting Will and his parents when a man they didn't know stopped his horse outside and came to the door. Samuel went to the door, leaving the others out of sight in the kitchen. They heard him explaining to Samuel that he carried hymnbooks in his saddlebags and wondered who might be interested in buying.

"Just trying to get a little money together," he said. "Got back from fighting, everything's gone. These were in a trunk out in the shed. My mother, rest her soul, was a great musician. Played every evening while I was growing up. I learned to love her tunes and selling these hymnbooks pure breaks my heart, but she would understand."

"Why are you trying to sell them here?" Samuel asked. "Sure be easier to find someone to buy in Asheville."

"Why, I want to bring some music to these people living back in the mountain valleys. I always was prone to think of the needy ones. You know anyone might be interested in these?"

"Not much money here in the valley to buy things."

"Well, know where me and my horse might could find a place to bed down for the night? It's a long way to go back out to Asheville."

"Why, you can stay here. I've got a room I'm building on. Thinking of starting a store folks can come to here at my mill. When I can get anything in to put on the shelves, of course. I'll just show you where to take your horse on down to the barn, and later I'll have my woman fix you up something to eat."

"Samuel hasn't said that many words at one time since we've been man and wife," Annie said in a low tone. "Something's not right. And that man coming all the way up here to sell hymnbooks."

"He's a bounty hunter," Will said grimly. "Someone sent out word. I wonder if it was Clyde McMillan."

Charity stood up. "We've got to get word to Daniel."

"Pa's taking him to the barn to give us time to get out. I'm sure of it. But now I can't get my horse."

"Come on, we'll borrow Nell's."

"No, Charity. I'll be less apt to let him see me and follow me to Daniel if I walk anyway. I've got to send Daniel up into the mountain somewhere. Then I'll stay in Daniel's house so when the bounty man gets the way from whoever sent for him, he'll find just me."

"Oh, I can't stand for Daniel to be up in the mountain, hunted and cold."

"I saw Mattie visiting Bethany and Joshua when I came back from cleaning at the church a little while ago," Annie said. "She can take him up on her mountain and hide him in a dozen places she knows up there where he'll be comfortable and no one can find him."

"I'll run over and be sure she doesn't go back up on the mountain before Daniel gets there," Charity said.

She and Will hurried out. "Will, be careful," she whispered.

Will almost grinned. "I think I'll enjoy this," he said. "We'll just wait out this man and his hymnbooks till he decides that he's in the wrong valley. And every time he comes up to Daniel's house, he'll find me. The hardest thing will be convincing Daniel to hide from him."

But Charity couldn't stop her frightened tears as she hurried to find Mattie. She ran into Bethany's house without taking time to knock, hardly able to talk. Bethany put her arms around her and calmed her down while Mattie listened stoically to her story.

"I'll put him in a cave I know," she said. "I stay there sometimes when I want to get out of my house and be close to the waterfall, so there's a sleeping place there."

Before long, Will and Daniel came. Charity ran to Daniel's arms. "Oh, Daniel, I was so afraid you wouldn't come," she whispered.

Daniel chuckled, as he hugged her. "I'm determined to live free here, Charity, but I'm not going to be stubbornly foolish." Then he sobered. "This will be the final test whether I can live here. Someone doesn't want me to or wants the money they promise. Will the rest of the people in the valley help hunt me down or support me? But, Charity, no matter which way it goes, you understand I had to take this chance."

Charity nodded reluctantly. "I think I do, Daniel."

"Daniel, you and Mattie need to go now," Bethany interrupted. "It will be a hard climb. I would send you up on Rainbow, but if anyone, friendly or not, sees her, they would know. . . . Mattie knows ways to walk up no one else does."

"I'll be fine. I've done a lot of mountain climbing lately." Daniel didn't explain whether he meant physically or spiritually.

Perhaps, Charity thought, *he meant both*.

twenty

"You're still here, Charity? Aren't you getting tired? Hungry?"

Charity looked up at Mattie, who looked like she was enjoying the dampness of her clothes from the mist around the waterfall. Then she realized that it was something far deeper than the mist that created the spiritual joy in Mattie's eyes. It must have come from Mattie's meditations in her retreat inside the cave.

She thought that perhaps now, in this mood and in this place where it had happened, Mattie would allow her to thank her for these things that meant so much to her. Mattie had always turned away with a look of embarrassment when she had tried before.

"Mattie, I want so much to thank you for taking care of Daniel those days while that horrible man looked for him."

"That man hadn't any idea how much I watched him hunt. And I stood outside every time he went up to Daniel's house and found Will livin' there. Saw him finally ride out after he couldn't get nobody to talk to him and decided that it was true Daniel'd gone to Canada and that coward who'd told on him had lied just to get his money. Could tell you who it was, too, but Daniel won't let me."

"I know. Daniel would rather just forgive him without knowing who." Charity had heard Mattie tell her story often before, but she knew how much pleasure Mattie got from talking about it, and listened quietly. "But I want to thank you for something else, too, Mattie. For talking to Will about forgiveness when he was struggling with his feelings about Daniel."

"Just did what my God wanted me to do," Mattie said. Then she shifted her bare feet closer to Charity. "Talkin' about forgivin', since you're the schoolmarm, maybe you can tell someone like me who never got the chance to learn to read, in words so's I can understand them, just what was the doins up in Washington City that lets Peter Matthews be Daniel Morgan again and livin' down in the valley free and easy like everyone else."

"Oh, Mattie, he was pardoned." Charity felt her own face glow with joy. Mattie waited quietly while she remembered a happy moment, then Charity got her thoughts together to make a simple explanation to this woman who was so wise in important things.

"After the war ended, the new president offered some Confederates a pardon if they would come back and promise to be faithful to the government, but Daniel wasn't included in that. He had owned property that was worth over a certain amount before the war. . . . I don't understand why that was important—"

Mattie swept her hand into a wide, dismissing circle.

"—and some of the bounty men still hadn't given up."

Mattie nodded, on a familiar subject now.

"At first we thought that there was no chance Daniel might be pardoned, then we heard that the president was giving out special pardons to some men who went to Washington to present their case. And Daniel decided to take a chance and go. You know that Dave went with him, of course. We were all so scared that he'd be recognized and thrown into jail before he got there."

An unusual smile lit Mattie's face. "A lot of people prayed that he wouldn't be. Maybe some prayed that he would. God knows. He's with us now."

Without explaining whether she was speaking of God's presence with them by the waterfall or Daniel's in the valley, and without saying any farewells, Mattie turned and left.

Charity watched her walk away, feeling deep affection for the woman. The happy thought came to her that she could repay some of Mattie's help to Daniel by offering to teach her to read.

When she returned to her memories, it was with a stronger feeling of gratitude for God's care for her and the people she loved. But the time of Daniel's trip to Washington City stayed in her mind.

Daniel had come down from the mountain to once again let the valley people choose whether or not to report him to the bounty hunters. He had remained totally open to them in his comings and goings, totally accepting of their judgment. And they had held their maker of music safe.

It was this that Charity mentally fell to her knees for each time she thought of it. Without the goodwill of the valley, the eventual amnesty of the government would not alone have made Daniel capable of forgiving himself and becoming the gift to the valley that he was capable of being.

All the while he and Dave were gone, Charity had gone to sleep and woke up in an agony of fear that only deep prayer could help, yet she felt that she grew more spiritually in that early spring month they were gone than in all her life before.

When they returned safely with the news that he was pardoned and a portion of their property returned to them, she was prompted to prayers of gratitude that were even more intense than her supplications had been before.

Soon after their celebration of his safety, Daniel spoke seriously with her.

"Charity, the land is in my name, but it is yours, too. My future is here. If you and Will want to go back to Tennessee, I'll deed the land to you. You can build a life there."

"Will belongs to the valley, Daniel. I won't even ask him to leave. One time when I was being ridiculous and calling him a Yankee who should leave, he told me he belonged here and he would never leave. I understand that now and I want to stay here, too."

"Very well, then. There are men wanting to buy land in that pleasant place. If you're sure, we'll sell."

"I'm sure, Daniel. I'm sure."

I'm sure, she thought now, feeling a fresh spray from the waterfall as a gentle breeze puffed by. *I'm so very sure of everything and so very happy.*

The noise of a horse coming up the mountainside caused Rainbow to sound a friendly whinny before she continued her eating. Charity rose and looked anxiously toward the trees.

She felt a happy glow leap into her eyes and her hands reached out to him as Will barely guided his horse away from the trees before he jumped off and came to her, his hands out to meet hers.

They simply touched their hands together for a long moment, then he pulled her closer, tenderly enclosing her shoulders and looking down at her.

"Charity Charlotte Morgan Soon-To-Be-Bowers, I don't ever quite believe that you're going to be my wife."

Charity looked deeply into his eyes, letting a glint of mischief show in hers. "I do. I do. I do. You see, I've been practicing my vows while you were gone."

He slipped his hands from her shoulders to her waist. "All right for you, but I don't need to practice. I do believe those words have been a part of me from the time you wandered into my private hideaway and refused to admit that you were lost or that you needed me. It took a snake and a cat and a bear—"

"And a storm. And a big decision on your part—"

"To make you admit that you need me." He stepped back, his hands still about her waist. "You do admit it, don't you?"

"I admit it. I glory in it. And it seemed like you were gone for months instead of days. Did you take care of Rance Hunt?"

"I did. He has the latest in wheelchairs and an appointment with the doctor to see if he can be fitted for peg legs. If he can't, they'll see if he can learn to swing himself along on crutches. And someday, when he's learned not to be so bitter, I may tell him that the money came from the sale of Daniel Morgan's land in Tennessee."

She threw her arms about his neck in exuberance. "Oh, Will, isn't it wonderful? When I came here, I didn't think my brother was even alive, and now he's been granted a pardon and. . .it's all right that he only got part of our land back. It doesn't matter. We're both part of this valley now. He wants to spend the rest of his life here and I do, too." She drew back and grinned up at Will. "And that trio he's made with Johnny Myers and Vern Rogers will sing at our wedding for their first time together."

"I can hardly wait, Charity-Charlotte-Morgan-Almost-Bowers."

Resting her head against his chest, she looked down at the leaf-lined mountainside below, letting her gaze move from a clump of mountain laurel to a spread of Queen Anne's lace and something purple-pink that she still must learn the name of.

"You know, the day you and I came into the valley last year, I told Joshua that these mountains dared me to love them, and he said that if I took the dare, I'd never want to leave. He was right. I want to live my life here. . .with you."

A Letter To Our Readers

Dear Reader:

In order that we might better contribute to your reading enjoyment, we would appreciate your taking a few minutes to respond to the following questions. We welcome your comments and read each form and letter we receive. When completed, please return to the following:

Rebecca Germany, Fiction Editor
Heartsong Presents
PO Box 719
Uhrichsville, Ohio 44683

1. Did you enjoy reading *Birdsong Road?*
   ☐ Very much. I would like to see more books
     by this author!
   ☐ Moderately
     I would have enjoyed it more if _____

   _____

   _____

2. Are you a member of **Heartsong Presents**? Yes ☐ No ☐
   If no, where did you purchase this book? _____

   _____

3. How would you rate, on a scale from 1 (poor) to 5 (superior),
   the cover design? _____

4. On a scale from 1 (poor) to 10 (superior), please rate the
   following elements.

   _____ Heroine   _____ Plot

   _____ Hero   _____ Inspirational theme

   _____ Setting   _____ Secondary characters

5. These characters were special because_____

_____

_____

6. How has this book inspired your life?_____

_____

_____

7. What settings would you like to see covered in future **Heartsong Presents** books?_____

_____

_____

8. What are some inspirational themes you would like to see treated in future books?_____

_____

_____

9. Would you be interested in reading other **Heartsong Presents** titles?   Yes ☐   No ☐

10. Please check your age range:
     ☐ Under 18   ☐ 18-24   ☐ 25-34
     ☐ 35-45   ☐ 46-55   ☐ Over 55

11. How many hours per week do you read?_____

Name _____

Occupation _____

Address _____

City _____ State _____ Zip _____

"How dreadfully old I'm getting!

Sixteen!" So begins *Stepping Heavenward* by Elizabeth Prentiss, the journal-like account of a nineteenth century girl who learns, on the path to womanhood, that true happiness can be found in giving oneself for others.

"This book is a treasure of both Godly and womanly wisdom told with disarming candor and humility, yet revealing a deep heart's desire to know God," says noted Christian speaker Elisabeth Elliot. "I do not hesitate to recommend it to men, who need to understand the wives they live with, and to any woman who wants to walk with God."

300 pages, Printed Leatherette, 4 $^{3}/_{16}$" x 6 $^{3}/_{4}$"

❤ ❤ ❤ ❤ ❤ ❤ ❤ ❤ ❤ ❤ ❤ ❤ ❤ ❤ ❤ ❤ ❤ ❤

❤ ❤ ❤ ❤ ❤ ❤ ❤ ❤ ❤ ❤ ❤ ❤ ❤ ❤ ❤ ❤ ❤ ❤

·····Hearts♥ng·····

HEARTSONG PRESENTS TITLES AVAILABLE NOW:

·········Presents·········

Great Inspirational Romance at a Great Price!

Heartsong Presents books are inspirational romances in contemporary and historical settings, designed to give you an enjoyable, spirit-lifting reading experience. You can choose wonderfully written titles from some of today's best authors like Peggy Darty, Sally Laity, Tracie Peterson, Colleen L. Reece, Lauraine Snelling, and many others.

When ordering quantities less than twelve, above titles are $2.95 each.
Not all titles may be available at time of order.

Heart♥ng Presents
Love Stories Are Rated G!

That's for godly, gratifying, and of course, great! If you love a thrilling love story, but don't appreciate the sordidness of some popular paperback romances, **Heartsong Presents** is for you. In fact, **Heartsong Presents** is the *only inspirational romance book club*, the only one featuring love stories where Christian faith is the primary ingredient in a marriage relationship.

Sign up today to receive your first set of four, never before published Christian romances. Send no money now; you will receive a bill with the first shipment. You may cancel at any time without obligation, and if you aren't completely satisfied with any selection, you may return the books for an immediate refund!

Imagine. . .four new romances every four weeks—two historical, two contemporary—with men and women like you who long to meet the one God has chosen as the love of their lives. . .all for the low price of $9.97 postpaid.

To join, simply complete the coupon below and mail to the address provided. **Heartsong Presents** romances are rated G for another reason: They'll arrive *Godspeed!*